DO NOT

DISTURB

A NOVEL BY

Freida McFadden

Do Not Disturb

ISBN: 9798474673417

This book is a work of fiction. The names, characters, incidents and places are the products of the authors' imagination, and are not to be construed as real. None of the characters in the book is based on an actual person. Any resemblance to persons living or dead is entirely coincidental and unintentional.

To Libby and Mel

NOVELS BY FREIDA McFADDEN

Do Not Disturb

The Locked Door

Want to Know a Secret?

One by One

The Wife Upstairs

The Perfect Son

The Ex

The Surrogate Mother

Brain Damage

Baby City

Suicide Med

The Devil Wears Scrubs

The Devil You Know

CHAPTER 1

QUINN

While I'm washing the blood off my hands in the kitchen sink, the doorbell rings.

I freeze, my hands full of pink suds, the steaming hot water causing my fingers to burn and tingle. There's somebody at the door. Somebody waiting patiently on the front porch for me to answer. The timing couldn't be worse.

Could it be a package delivery? Maybe they'll drop the package at the door and go away. Or else leave me a note. *Sorry we missed you! We'll be back tomorrow!*

And then: three hard raps on the front door.

"Coming!" I call out in a strangled voice, even though it's unlikely they'll hear me. I scrub furiously at my fingers, and then at my fingernails, where the blood seems to have settled into the cracks. Who knew it was so hard to get blood off your hands? "Just a minute!"

I shut off the hot water and examine my palms, flipping them this way and that. Good enough? It'll have to be. I wipe them dry on a light green dish towel, leaving a smear of red behind. Damn, I didn't get it all—I'll have to wash my hands again.

As soon as I get rid of whoever is at the front door.

My heels clack against the linoleum floor of the kitchen, then go soft when they hit the plush carpeting in the living room. Derek and I pored over carpet swatches for hours before settling on the charcoal-colored carpet that now goes wall-to-wall across our vast living room. The carpet feels lovely when I'm in my bare feet, and I'm glad I held out for a darker color instead of a pale shade that would show every fleck of dirt. Our carpet can easily hide dust and debris.

Bloodstains too, apparently.

As I hurry to the front door, I glimpse bright lights through the windows. Red and blue flashing simultaneously. That can mean only one thing.

There's a cop at my door.

Oh God. No no no no no…

I take a split second to compose myself. *Keep it together, Quinn.* I take a deep breath, trying to get my hands to stop shaking. It doesn't work. So I go ahead and open the door.

I was right. It's a police officer at my door. Not just a police officer, but it's Scotty Dwyer, although he goes by Scott now, or else Deputy Dwyer. About a million years ago, when we were in high school, Scott and I used to date. I remember how awkwardly cute I thought he was, with his red-brown hair that always stuck up straight and all the freckles on his face. But then high school ended, I went off to college, and he went to work for his father's grocery store. I don't even remember breaking up with him, but the long-distance phone calls became less frequent, and one day during my freshman year, I realized we weren't together anymore.

Now Scotty is a policeman with a uniform and a real badge and everything. He used to be skinny as a rail, but now he fills out his dark blue uniform rather nicely. The freckles have faded, and he's tamed his hair, although he still looks boyishly handsome.

That's the problem with moving back to the town where I grew up. Everyone I run into is the boy I went out with in high school or the kid who saw me throw up in the locker room or the girl who didn't invite me to her birthday party. It's exhausting.

But sometimes it can work to my advantage.

"Hey, Quinn." Scott smiles at me, but his face is serious. This isn't a social call—not that I would have expected it, since I have barely spoken to Scott in the last ten years. "Is everything okay?"

I wipe my hands self-consciously on my gray pencil skirt. "Sure. Of course. Why?"

"Well…" Scott's light brown eyes dart behind me, scanning my living room. The buttery leather sofa, the matching loveseat and ottoman, the wide screen television with surround sound, the photographs on our mantle of our recent skiing trip to Vale. "We got a phone call. One of your neighbors said they heard screaming coming from your house."

"Screaming?" I paste what I think is a very realistic looking smile on my face. "That's so strange! Are they sure it was coming from here?"

His eyes lock with mine. "That's what they said, yes."

I screw up my face, pretending to think about it. Finally, I snap my fingers. "Oh! You know what it was? I was watching a movie on TV, and then I went out to the kitchen and I turned the volume way up. So they probably heard the movie."

He nods, considering this. Everyone says Scott is a good policeman—kind but thorough. I squeeze my hands into fists, waiting to see if he buys my story. I look down at my trembling hands again, scared they might give me away. And that's when I notice it.

A crimson dot on my gray skirt.

Oh God, how did I miss it? How did I let myself answer the door with a drop of blood on my skirt? I quickly avert my eyes, trying not to draw attention to it. If he sees it, he'll insist on coming inside. And if he does, I'm finished.

"What movie?" he finally asks.

"Well," I say, "it was *Scream*. You know, with Neve Campbell and Courteney Cox?"

He clears his throat. "The one with the masks, right?"

"Right. So obviously, there was, you know, *screaming*." I smile apologetically. "I'm sorry if somebody got worried. But you can see there's no disturbance here."

"Uh huh…"

I hold my breath, keeping my eyes pointed straight ahead. I send Scott a subliminal message: *Don't look down. Please don't look down.*

Scott tilts his head to the side. "Are you alone here?"

I play with my hair, trying for casual and flirty. Easy, breezy. *Nothing to see here, Officer.* "Yep. Just little ol' me. Derek is still at work."

Don't look down. Please…

Finally, he nods his head. "Okay. Sorry to bother you. I just wanted to make sure everything was all right."

"Of course!" I laugh, hoping it doesn't sound as weird to him as it does to me. "I'm glad you came. It makes me feel safe to know you're out there protecting me."

Scott's cheekbones turn just the slightest bit pink. When we were in high school and he was embarrassed, his whole face would turn scarlet. "Just doing my job."

"I appreciate it. And next time, I promise I'll keep the

volume down. Especially when I'm watching scary movies!"

He wags a finger at me. "You do that."

"And we should catch up sometime," I add. "Derek and I would love to have you over for dinner."

"Sounds great, Quinn."

Scott doesn't want to have dinner with me and Derek. But that's fine, since it wasn't a genuine invitation, anyway.

He ambles down my front steps, and then down my driveway to his parked police car with the flashing red and blue lights. I never quite meant to break up with Scotty Dwyer, but now, for the first time, I wonder what my life would have been like if I hadn't. If I had married a good, honorable man of the law instead of Derek, the man that I chose. I wouldn't be standing here with blood on my skirt and on the soles of my shoes. That much is for sure.

I shut the door, but I keep watching Scott through the front window. I watch as he starts up the engine and pulls onto the road, and I don't look away until his car is out of sight.

He's gone. Thank God.

Now that he's out of sight, I inspect my skirt. The drop of blood is about half a centimeter in diameter. I've never attempted to get blood out of my clothing before, but I have a bad feeling my best work skirt is ruined. Then again, that's the least of my problems.

I walk back out to the kitchen, examining the carpet for signs of bloody footprints. The kitchen looks about the same as how I left it a few minutes ago. The sink faucet is dripping like it always does. There's still that crimson smear on the green dish towel. The three plates I left in the drying rack are still lined up in a row. The refrigerator has that note taped up that I wrote to myself to remember to buy more paper towels.

And also, my husband is still lying dead on the kitchen floor in a pool of blood.

CHAPTER 2

I want to make one thing clear. I killed him.

I'm not going to claim it was the butler or a one-armed man. I did it. I killed my husband. All I can say in my defense is I had a good reason.

I look down at Derek, lying where I left him on the kitchen floor, his warm blood forming an uneven circle under his body. The knife is next to him, also dripping with blood and covered with my fingerprints. For a moment, I consider wiping the handle clean, but what would I be trying to achieve? This is my house. Nobody has as good a motive for killing Derek as I do. I tracked my own bloody footprints all over the carpet. Oh, and a police officer just saw me here at what I'm sure will be the approximate time of Derek's death.

So I would say a few fingerprints are not worth

worrying about.

I bend down beside him, getting more blood on my skirt, but I think we can assume the skirt is a lost cause at this point. His brown eyes are cracked open as he stares into nothingness, his perfectly chiseled features frozen. The muscles in his face are completely relaxed for the first time since I've known him. Even when Derek is sleeping, he's tense. He grinds his teeth loud enough to wake me. Maybe in death, he's achieved that total relaxation that the meditation app on his phone failed to provide. Maybe he's finally achieved a sublime state of complete bliss.

Would it be a terrible thing to say that I hope he *hasn't* achieved bliss? Would it be terrible to say that I hope he's burning in hell right now?

Well, either way, it's true.

And now I have to figure out my next move. As I see it, I've got two options:

1) Stay here and confess
2) Run

Option number one is tempting. After all, I'm already here. Inertia is powerful. And perhaps I could spin this. After all, my neighbor heard me screaming. Would anyone believe it if I told them the truth? That if Derek weren't lying here dead, it would have been me. Him or me—that's what it came down to.

I reach out and touch my neck. It's still tender from where his fingers were. There will be bruises. He's never left behind bruises before—at least not in a place anyone else could see. I can still hear his voice hissing in my face: *Why are you home so early? Who were you planning to meet here?*

Him or me. Maybe a jury would sympathize.

Then again, it's not likely. Derek was well-liked by everyone in our community and also *connected*. He owns a business that everyone in New England has heard of. And more importantly, his *family* is connected. They've donated to every state politician currently in office, including the DA. And they never liked me. If they find out what I've done, they won't rest until I'm rotting away in a prison cell for the rest of my life. They will spend every penny they've got to make me pay for this.

So that leaves one option: *Run.*

I don't want to leave my home. Or my job at the bank. My parents are gone, but my older sister Claudia lives only twenty minutes away, and she would be devastated if I disappeared off the face of the earth. But she would understand. She knows about Derek. What he's like.

It's Friday afternoon. If the odds are in my favor, nobody will find out about this until Monday, when neither of us show for work. Of course, that precludes the possibility that Deputy Dwyer pays us another visit. Or my sister pops in to say hello. Or more likely, Derek's mother comes by for *absolutely no reason at all* except to count all the ways I'm an unsatisfactory wife. (To be fair, this time she would be absolutely right.)

I get up off the floor and look down at my husband's body. If somebody comes into this house, I'm done. They will see him immediately, and the manhunt will begin. Derek's mother has a key, because she likes to come in anytime she wants. The chances of me getting a three day head start are small. But maybe I'll get twenty-four hours.

Of course, if things had gone differently, and I was the one lying on the ground right now, Derek could easily lift me up, throw me in his trunk, and toss me in a nearby body of water. Then he could come home and clean up the evidence. But I can't do that. Derek has a good eighty pounds on me. There's no way I could lift his body. He died on the kitchen floor and that's where he's staying. Attempting to do anything else will waste valuable time.

No, if I'm going to run, I've got to run right now.

But first, I have to change.

I run upstairs to our bedroom. I made the bed this morning, the way Derek likes, with our Seraphina Ivory Damask bedspread folded neatly over the bed and the pillows propped up and fluffed. My mother always had me make the bed when I was a kid, but I stopped doing it as an adult. Until I got married, and I realized Derek required it. And it didn't just have to be made—it had to be made in a very particular way, according to his specifications.

I flash back to a moment a couple of months ago, when

Derek walked into our bedroom and discovered that I had folded the bedspread *over* the pillows, rather than under. He narrowed his eyes as I felt my stomach sink.

So this is how you leave our house in the morning? he said. *Looking like a pigsty?*

To be fair, the rest of the house was immaculate. I had cleaned every inch myself, because Derek did not want to hire a housekeeper. He hated the idea of having a stranger in our house and insisted it was my responsibility. So in addition to my full-time job, I did all the cooking and cleaning and shopping.

I push aside the memory of the way Derek screamed at me that day. I stare down at the blankets on the bed, seized by a sudden irrepressible urge to mess them up, just to spite him.

But no. No time for that. I spited him enough by murdering him.

Even though there's precious little time, I spend ten minutes stripping off all my clothing and jumping into the hot shower. There's so much blood in the kitchen. More blood than I thought possible for somebody to have in their body, and I can't risk having a drop on me. Wherever I end up, I have to look sweet and innocent. Bloody hands and crimson-speckled cheeks are not an option.

I turn the shower up as hot as it can go. Scalding. I let the water run over me, immune to the pain. Every time I shut my eyes, I see him coming at me.

You've made a fool out of me for the last time, Quinn.

His fingers closing around my neck, compressing my windpipe. Flailing around with my right hand until it made contact with the knife rack on the kitchen counter…

I swallow, and with trembling fingers, I turn up the water temperature as hot as it will go. My nerve endings are screaming, but I welcome it.

When I get out of the shower, my skin is bright red. I wrap a towel around my body and stare at myself in the mirror over the sink. Unsurprisingly, I don't look great. My eyes are sunken in their sockets. My blond hair is plastered to my skull, cascading down my shoulders in limp clumps. Even though it's wet, I can see the dark roots growing in— he pointed it out to me last night. *Time to get to the hairdresser, Quinn.* When I first met Derek, my hair was shoulder length and brown, but he liked my hair long and blond. But even after years of being blond, it never felt like me.

Well, that's one thing I can change now.

I can't do anything about the color—at least not yet— but it doesn't have to be so long. I pick up the pair of scissors from inside the medicine cabinet. Before I can overthink it, I slice my hair off at chin length. I don't spend too much time making sure it's even, and also, my hands won't stop shaking, which doesn't help matters. The entire process takes about sixty seconds. I flush all the hair down the toilet so nobody will know I did it.

There. I look a lot different with my hair so short. It's not enough, but it's a start.

I pack a bag as rapidly as I can—I toss in some shirts, bras, underwear, and pants. I take all my jewelry, figuring I could hock it if I need to. I also open the shoe box in the back of the closet where I've been stashing money whenever I can, as well as my passport. Somehow I knew I would need it for a day like today. The money isn't much, but it will get me through a few weeks, at least. I can also hit an ATM or two, but I have to be careful about that. Every time I withdraw money, I'll be leaving a trail the police will follow.

I get a sick feeling just thinking about it. This is my life from now on. Hiding from the police. I'll never see my home again. I'll never see my sister again.

But it's that or life in prison.

After my bag is packed, I hesitate at the top of the stairwell, my stomach fluttering. I was up there too long. Too many wasted minutes. What if Scott came back to check on me? What if he didn't really believe I was watching the movie *Scream*?

What if the first floor of my house is crawling with cops, waiting to drag me away in cuffs?

My sensible sneakers thump on the steps. I take them slowly, watching to see if anyone is waiting for me. My heart is pounding. I was stupid to spend so much time up there. I should have grabbed whatever I could and run.

But the living room is silent. Just like I left it.

Thank God.

I won't make the same mistake again. I don't bother to look around the living room and make sure I've gotten every last thing. Everything I own is expendable. Anyway, what would I take? A picture of me and Derek from one of our trips? No way. I want to forget his perfect, handsome, smug face.

So instead, I go straight to the garage. My blue Toyota Corolla is sitting there, waiting for me. We have a two-car garage and Derek's Porsche is right next to my Corolla. He never understood why I didn't want a fancy, expensive car like he had. Why would I keep the same crappy Corolla I drove back when I was single?

He didn't get it. This car is *mine*. I paid for it myself, unlike our ridiculously extravagant house and furnishings. It's the last thing I own that still feels like me.

I climb in my Corolla and start up the engine.

And I run.

CHAPTER 3

I have no idea where I'm going.

It's not like I did this with any kind of well-thought-out plan. I didn't wake up this morning and say to myself, *Hey, I'm going to kill my husband today!* If I had done something like that, I would have filled up my gas tank beforehand, for starters.

I also would have picked a better day to do it, weather-wise. December has been unseasonably warm this year, but of course, today would be the day we get blessed with freezing rain. That lovely combination of rain and snow is slowly coating the roads and obscuring my windshield as I travel as fast as I dare. And all the while, the sun is dropping in the sky, making it harder and harder to see.

It's like Derek is already haunting me from beyond the

grave.

But I've got to keep going. I have to put as many miles as I can between me and the house where I murdered my husband. Because I don't have long.

I'm going to head north. I need to get out of the country. And I'm far closer to Canada than I am to Mexico. Hopefully at the border, they won't look too carefully at my passport and just wave me through.

I've been driving less than twenty minutes when my phone rings. The display in my car pops up the name Claudia Delaney.

It's my sister.

I hesitate, not sure if I should take the call. It's not that I don't have some friends and coworkers that I like, but the only person I'll really miss will be Claudia. She's four years older than me, and she's always looked out for me, especially after our parents died when I was only fourteen. When she finds out what happened, she's going to be worried sick.

I've got to talk to her one last time. I need to let her know I'm all right.

I press the button to take the call. "Hi, Claudia!" I say in a voice that is so ridiculously chipper, I'm convinced she'll know instantly something is wrong.

"Hey, Quinn," she says. "Where are you? Are you free?"

I almost laugh at how ridiculous the question is. "Not

at the moment. I'm… still at work."

"What time do you get off? Do you want to grab dinner?"

"No, I…" I squeeze the steering wheel until my knuckles turn white. "I have to work late tonight."

"Again?" She lets out a huff. "They work you way too hard at the bank."

"Yeah," I mumble.

Claudia clucks her tongue. "Tell you what. How about if I come over tonight with a bottle of wine? We can watch something on Netflix."

"No!" The light turns red, and I have to jam my foot on the brake to keep from crashing into the car in front of me. That's all I need right now. "I mean… I've got a headache and I… it's not a good night. I don't feel like socializing."

There's a long silence on the other line. "Quinn, are you okay?"

"Fine!" My voice cracks on the word, and I have to clear my throat. "I'm totally fine, Claudia. Really."

"Are you sure?"

I grip the steering wheel tighter, picturing my sister's round face, Cupid's bow lips, and dark hair cut into a bob. I wish I could tell her the truth. I want more than anything to tell Claudia what happened and what I've done. If there's any person in the world who would understand, it's her.

But if I tell her the truth, she's going to try to convince

me to come back. She doesn't want to lose me, so she'll tell me to come home. And that's the wrong thing to do. She doesn't know the extent of the connections Derek's family has. And even though she doesn't like Derek, she doesn't really understand quite how bad he is. I've been afraid to tell her all the details, because I thought she would beat him to death with a rolling pin—she's very protective of me. And truthfully, I didn't understand *quite* how bad he was until today.

"I'm fine," I say. "I promise."

"Do you triple dipper promise with a cherry on top?"

That's something we always used to say when we were kids. Because the ice cream store down the block had a triple dipper cone with a cherry on top, and it was our favorite. "Yes. I triple dipper promise with a cherry on top."

"Fine." I hear the pout in her voice. "But you owe me dinner out. Tomorrow night, Rob and I are going out... how about Sunday?"

I swallow. I can't agree to Sunday. Because when I don't show up, she'll go to my house. I don't want her to be the one to discover Derek's body—I can't do that to her. "How about Monday?"

"Deal. Let's meet at Donatello's at seven. Don't be late!"

"I won't." I hesitate, desperately wanting to say the words, *I love you*. Claudia is my only family, and I may never see her again. I want to tell her I love her, but if I do, she will for sure know something is wrong. It's not the typical way we end conversations. So instead, I say, "Bye, Claudia."

"Bye! Remember—don't keep me waiting!"

We end the call, and I sit there for a moment, staring at the freezing rain hitting my windshield.

"I love you, Claudia," I say to the windshield.

And then I start to cry.

———

Ironically, the first time I met Derek, I wasn't attracted to him at all.

It's strange because of... well, how handsome he is. *Was*, I should say. He walked into our little New Hampshire bank, lighting up the entire room with his gleaming chestnut hair, deep brown eyes, and perfectly chiseled features. He filled out his Armani suit like he was poured into it. Every item I owned in the world combined, including my freaking *car*, was worth less than that suit.

Melody, who sat at the desk next to mine, nudged me hard and licked her lips. I was secretly hoping Derek would sit down in front of Melody's desk. But no. He chose mine.

Derek explained his situation to me. His family owned a rather large Boston-based business and was looking to expand to the rest of New England. When he said the name of the company, my mouth fell open. My first instinct was that our bank was too small and he was too big a fish. But he was hoping for the personalized service that our small bank would provide.

That is to say, he hoped we would fall all over ourselves to help him.

The vice president of the bank came out to meet with him personally. When he found out that I was the one dealing with Derek, he gave me a meaningful look. *Be really nice to this one, Quinn.*

So when I had finished setting up an account for Derek and he asked me out for drinks after work, I said yes. After all, I had to be *nice.*

I was single at the time. And Derek was so nice and charming when we went out for drinks. I didn't quite trust him, because how could you trust somebody with so much money who looked like *that?* You would have to be stupid not to have a healthy dose of skepticism. But over the evening, he wore me down. When he asked if I would have dinner with him on Saturday night, I agreed.

Only six months later, he asked me to marry him. Six months after that, we tied the knot. The entire year, it was like floating on a cloud. Derek was the most wonderful man I had ever met.

It wasn't until after we were husband and wife that everything changed.

Derek had been shopping for a new bank, but in retrospect, what he really had been shopping for was a wife. He took one look at me and decided I fit the bill. I still don't know what it was about me that drew him to me. Or maybe it was all just dumb luck. Maybe if he had sat in front of Melody's desk, she would be the one now speeding towards the state line.

I wish it could have been different. I wish Derek had been the man he promised to be. Or better yet, I wish I had listened to Claudia and stayed the hell away from him.

But it's too late now. I have no choice but to play with the cards I've been dealt.

CHAPTER 4

The gas tank is just about empty. There are usually twelve dots on the gas gauge, and I'm down to the last dot. I don't know how long one dot will last, and I don't want to know. I need to get some gas—now.

I've been on the highway for about half an hour, and I look for signs for the next rest stop. I'm looking for the tiny signs—the stops where almost nobody gets off, where I'm least likely to be spotted. Not that I think anybody is looking for me yet, but I don't know for sure.

When I see the tiny sign for Rocco's Gas Station, I pull off the highway. When I drive into the two pump station, I'm relieved to see it's exactly what I'm looking for. A quiet little self service station, with a tiny store attached and an elderly man sitting at the counter. There's only one other car at the station—a gray pickup truck that looks like it's seen better days.

I park my car at the remaining pump and pop the lid for the gas tank. I zip up my black coat and throw on my hood, then step out into the cold. Droplets of freezing rain immediately smack me in the face. I barely feel it though. I'm not feeling much of anything anymore.

You've made a fool out of me for the last time, Quinn.

I can hear his last words so loudly, it's like he is speaking in my ear. I can't stop imagining Derek coming at me. The rage on his face. He was convinced I was cheating on him, even though I never looked at another man. I was too scared to even *talk* to another man. Once Derek came to see me at the bank, and he "caught" me talking to an attractive male client—he was beyond furious about it that night. It didn't help that Derek himself had once been my client. Ever since then, I tried to send any male customers who weren't elderly over to one of my coworkers.

But I'm safe now. He can't get to me.

Never again.

I insert my credit card, select regular, and fill up my tank. This will be the last time I use my credit card. There's an ATM in the gas station store, and I'm going to take out as much money as it will let me. Then that's it. I'm going off the grid.

After my tank is full, I look into the store. That old

man is still behind the counter, and the owner of the truck is moving around inside the store. I dig around inside my pocket and pull out my cell phone. I keep my eyes on the store as I drop the phone into the back of a pickup truck, below a blue tarp. I don't know if anyone can track me with my phone, but if they do, they'll track me to wherever this guy is going. Maybe that will buy me some time.

The first thing I see when I get into the store is the television monitor set up behind the counter. The old man is watching it to entertain himself. It's tuned in to the local news.

"Lousy weather we're having, eh?" the old man says. There's a glob of drool in the corner of his mouth.

I offer him a ghost of a smile. "Yes…"

I stand there for a moment, trying to decide if I should take my hood off or not. The hood conceals my hair and some of my face. But then again, I don't want him to remember me as the lunatic walking around with a furry hood on indoors. After a moment of deliberation, I leave it on.

There are some sandwiches set up in a refrigerated area, but I don't know about eating egg salad from the gas station store. This egg salad might be older than I am. Instead, I stick with grabbing a few packs of trail mix and nutrition bars. Then I see a pack of cheese doodles. I love cheese doodles. I don't think I've eaten cheese doodles in the last two years. Derek kept a close eye on what I ate.

Stuffing your face again, Quinn? You're getting pretty chunky.

During dinner with some friends of his, he became enraged when I ordered a chocolate mousse for dessert. He marched me to the bathroom scale when we got home, and after that, we did regular weigh-ins. He would write the number each week in a little notebook. As I would step on the scale, I would hold my breath, knowing if my weight was even a pound higher than last week, he would go crazy.

I put back the trail mix and nutrition bars. Instead, I grab the cheese doodles and a pack of Oreos. To hell with Derek. He's dead anyway.

Before I pay for my purchases, I hit the ATM. My fingers are shaking as I type in my PIN number. The upper limit on withdrawals is only two hundred dollars. Not enough, although it will have to be. Dammit.

As I'm pulling out my cash, I feel a pair of eyes on my back. I glance behind me—it's a guy around twenty-five who's nearly a foot taller than me with arms and legs like tree trunks. He's probably the owner of the pickup truck. He flashes me a smile, and I nod as imperceptibly as I can.

I go to the refrigerator and grab a couple of bottles of water, but I still feel his eyes on my back. Derek was always accusing men of staring at me, but right now I'm wearing a big puffy coat and my hood is on. Why is he looking at me?

I don't need this right now. I need to get out of the store and back on the road.

I'm juggling my water, cheese doodles, and the Oreos as I make my way to the counter. The large man follows me, his boots squishing as they make wet footprints on the ground. This time I don't turn to look at him.

I dump all my purchases on the counter. And I grab a couple of Twix bars for good measure. I'll pay with my credit card this one last time. I already used it at the gas station, so I might as well.

"That all?" the old man behind the counter asks me.

I nod. The gaze of the man behind me is boring into me. I've got to get out of here.

While the old man rings up my purchases, I glance at the television screen. It's still tuned to the news. The local news. I hold my breath as I wait to hear what stories they announce. They're talking about some sort of problem with the school heating system. That's good. They wouldn't be talking about a bunch of heaters if they found a dead body in a local couple's house.

But it's just a matter of time. They're going to find him.

"Here you go." The man slides a paper bag with my purchases across the counter at me. His eyes dip down to look at the name on my credit card. "Have a good day, Quinn."

I flinch at the mention of my name. But it's fine. I'm getting back on the road, and by the time the police track me to this place, I'll be long gone.

But as I head for the door, so does the man from the

pickup truck. He's following me.

I rifle around in my pocket for my keys. All I can do is get to my car as quickly as I can. The old man is still watching, so it's not like the guy is going to attack me.

As I step outside, a gush of cold smacks me in the face. It must've gotten at least ten degrees colder while I was in that store. The rain hasn't quite turned into snow yet, but it will soon. How much longer can I stay on the road?

And what's worse, I can hear the man's footsteps behind me.

I quicken my pace. I don't know what he wants, but it can't be anything good. There are about twenty feet between me and my car. I've just got to make it twenty feet. I hit the key fob and my car lights up. Almost there.

But then a brawny hand grabs my shoulder.

CHAPTER 5

"Quinn?"

He knows my name. This random stranger at a gas station is calling me by my name. Of course, the old man read it off my credit card, so he might've heard him. But as I whirl around to confront him, I see the recognition on his face.

"Quinn, right?" he says again.

"Um…" I look down at my plastic bag of groceries, then back up at his face. Despite the man's size, there's nothing menacing about his facial expression. "Yes…"

He grins at me. "I'm Bill Walsh. *Billy.* You used to babysit for me."

My mouth falls open. That was the absolute last thing I expected him to say. "Oh."

He rubs his hands together. "Do you remember me?"

I babysat a lot of kids when I was a teenager. The name

Billy Walsh sounds mildly familiar. But I'm guessing this hulking man looks a lot different than he did when he was a kid. "Sure," I lie.

His eyes light up. "You were my favorite babysitter. You always let me have as many cookies as I wanted."

I'm not sure if that's the way I want to be remembered, but it could be worse. But it's troubling that even with my hair a different color than when I was younger and hacked into a bob and a hood mostly concealing it, he *still* recognized me. Apparently, I'm not quite as incognito as I had hoped.

"Also…" His eyes twinkle. "I had a *huge* crush on you. I bet you knew."

It's cold and raining, and all I want is to get back on the road. "No, I didn't."

"Huh." He scratches at the back of his head. He's not wearing a hood like I am or even a hat. Isn't he cold? "Well, anyway, maybe we can get together sometime. Catch up on old times?"

My cheeks burn. I can't believe this. I stopped at a gas station in the middle of nowhere, and suddenly I'm having a conversation with a kid I babysat for fifteen years ago, who is now inexplicably asking me out on a date.

"Actually," I say, "I'm moving up to Vermont. So I won't be local anymore." I shrug. "But it was nice seeing you again, Billy."

His face falls. "Oh. But maybe I could get your number

and—"

"Sorry," I say.

Without waiting for a response, I turn and walk the rest of the way to my car. I don't hazard a look behind me until I'm at the driver's side door. He's still standing there, watching me.

Damn, I wish I hadn't thrown my phone in his pickup truck. I had been hoping he was some guy from way out of town, in the opposite direction of where I wanted to go. I wanted that phone to take the police on a wild goose chase. But if he's headed back where I come from, it will take them all of five minutes to figure out my phone is in the back of his truck.

Worse, he'll be able to give the police an updated description of me. He can tell them I cut my hair. All the more reason I have to get hair dye as soon as possible. And maybe I need to hack my hair off a bit shorter. I always wanted a pixie cut. I almost laugh as I imagine the look on Derek's face if I had come home with a pixie cut. But it wouldn't have been funny back then. Not even a little.

As I pull onto the road, Billy Walsh is still staring after me. No, he's definitely not going to forget me. I made a huge mistake pulling over here.

Maybe I should head back. It's not too late. I could go home and confess to the police what I did. It's better if I confess than if they discover it themselves. Better than trying to escape during what is possibly turning into a blizzard.

But I don't turn around.

———

At about five-thirty, the sun dropped precipitously in the sky. By two hours into my drive, it's pitch black. I can just hardly see the road in front of me with my windshield wipers going full blast. I'm the only car on the road, so I put on my brights. If I get in a car wreck, I'm finished.

I don't know what to do. I had hoped to keep driving for at least seven or eight hours without stopping, but the Corolla won't make it much further. I wish I had bought a bigger car. But who knew I'd be fleeing a murder scene?

I suspect the right thing to do is to pull off the highway. Find a quiet place and sleep in the car. I've got my cheese doodles and my Oreos, which isn't exactly nourishing, but it will get me through the night. But where can I pull over around here?

If Claudia were here, she would tell me what to do.

I get a deep ache in my chest as I think about my big sister. I can't believe I'm never going to see her again. She's the only reason I'm even considering going back. She always knows what to do. After our parents died, she put her arm around me at the funeral and said, *Don't worry, Quinn. I'll take care of you.*

And she did. She left college and won guardianship of me. We had little family, and if she hadn't stepped in, I would have had to go live with some distant relatives I had never met. Or lived in foster care. I owe Claudia everything.

We used to talk about Derek a lot. I would tell her carefully edited versions of some things he said to me. I was careful not to tell her about the bruises he left behind when he grabbed my arm or the times he pulled my hair. Even with the washed down version, she was furious. She told me I should leave him. But she didn't get it. Derek wasn't just rich—he was *powerful*. If I left him, he would make sure I never worked in banking ever again. He told me I would spend the rest of my life penniless and miserable. Although some days, that felt better than the alternative.

And of course, after one of our huge fights, Derek would always fall over himself to apologize. There would be flowers, expensive jewelry, maybe a dinner out at a nice restaurant. He would be nice for weeks until I forgot the fight and remembered the man I had fallen in love with. So I stayed.

When I was younger, before I met Derek, I would hear stories about women stuck in abusive relationships. I never understood why any of them stayed. I thought they were foolish or weak. It never made sense to me until it became my life.

Over the sound of the engine and the wind and rain outside, I hear another noise. It takes me a second to make it out. But when I do, my stomach sinks.

It's a siren.

CHAPTER 6

There's a police car in my rearview mirror, flashing its lights. There are no other cars on the road. The police officer wants me to stop.

Oh no. Have they discovered the body already?

Maybe Scotty Dwyer didn't believe my story as much as I thought he did. Maybe after another hour, he went back to our house. He would have noticed the windows were dark inside. And then what? Would he have busted down the door to see what was inside? That seems extreme.

But he could have discovered the key we always keep under the potted plant by the back door. Scott is smart enough to check the obvious places.

My hands tighten on the steering wheel until my knuckles go white. I wish Scott had insisted on looking around. He would have discovered the body, and I could have told him everything that happened. Scott was so kind to me when we were younger—he would have believed me.

He would have known I'm not a murderer.

But it's worse now. I fled the scene of the crime. The more distance I put between myself and Derek's body, the more guilty I look.

There's no chance of a high-speed chase right now. I pull over to the side of the road as carefully as I can. The police car pulls over behind me. I sit there for a moment, my heart pounding so hard, it hurts. I might have a heart attack right now. I almost hope I do. It would be easier than dealing with what's going to happen next.

The police officer takes his sweet time getting out of the vehicle. I had been hoping it might be Scott, but it isn't. It's somebody I don't know. He's a large man with a shaved head, dressed in a dark uniform, and he's got an umbrella in his right hand as he makes his way to my car. Somehow, the umbrella makes him seem a little less scary.

Until he raps hard on the window of my car.

I roll down the window. Immediately, bits of icy rain smack me in the face. I do my best to smile, even though I am about to pee in my pants.

"Hi, Officer," I say. "Um, everything okay?"

In the shadows, I can just barely make out the lines in his face. "I wouldn't have stopped you if it were, would I? Let's see your license, Miss."

My hands are shaking as I reach for my purse. It takes me two tries to get my wallet open and slide out my driver's license. I almost drop it as I try to hand it to him.

"Quinn Alexander." He reads my name off my license, then looks up to match the picture with my face. "A bit of a way from home, aren't you?"

I shrug. "I'm, uh… visiting some friends."

"I see. Awfully bad weather for a road trip."

"Yeah, kind of." I swallow a hard lump in my throat. "Look, Officer, I couldn't have been speeding. I've been going well under the speed limit."

He waits for a beat. "That isn't why I pulled you over."

"Oh…" I wrack my brain, trying to think of something I might have done wrong. I mean, other than murdering a man a few hours ago. "I… I don't understand."

The officer nods at the back of my vehicle. "You got a busted tail light. On the left."

Is that it? Thank God. "Do I?"

"Yeah." He frowns at me. "When it's this dark out, a broken tail light can kill you. A car might be behind you and just see the one light, and maybe they think you're a motorcycle or who knows what. I've seen some nasty accidents happen because of broken tail lights. I won't give you a ticket, but you need to get it fixed as soon as possible. For your own safety."

"Oh…" I nod soberly. "I'll be sure to take care of it right away."

"Are you almost at your friend's house?"

"Yes. Just about."

He hands me back my driver's license. "You need to

get off the road—soon. With this storm and now your busted tail light… It's an accident waiting to happen."

"Right. I understand."

"The next time I see you, I don't want it to be in a body bag."

I can't help but think of Derek. Have they discovered him yet? No, they couldn't have. If they had, this police officer wouldn't be letting me go.

I almost can't believe it when the officer walks back to his car. He didn't arrest me. I'm still free. But for how long?

I pull back onto the road, recognizing that the first chance I've got, I have to change course and go in a completely different direction. Once they start searching for me, the officer will remember me. He'll remember what direction I was headed in.

But for now, I've got a bigger problem. If I keep driving around with this broken tail light, I'll get pulled over again. The next time I might not be so lucky. I've got to get off the road. Just for the night, and then I can start driving again in the morning. Nobody will notice a broken tail light in the daytime.

And that's when I see the sign on the side of the road. It's so tiny that I almost miss it. And that's perfect.

The Baxter Motel. That's where I'll spend the night, then tomorrow bright and early, I'll get back on the road.

CHAPTER 7

If I were looking for a quiet, isolated place to spend the night, I couldn't find anything more quiet and isolated than the Baxter Motel. I turn off the highway, and an almost invisible sign directs me to the motel. I have to drive down a nearly unpaved road until I see the weather-worn sign in front of a beat up old two-story house with a crumbling porch. The roof looks warped, almost sunken, like it could collapse at any moment. There's a dim light shining in one of the upstairs windows, and if there weren't, I would think the motel was abandoned.

Even though it's isolated, I feel nervous about parking my car in plain sight. After all, that officer pulled me over only twenty minutes away from here.

Next to the motel, there's another small one-story building. There's a sign hanging from it that says Rosalie's

Diner in peeling paint. But this establishment is clearly closed. It's dark inside and all the windows and doors are boarded up. I circle around the diner, and I park behind it, concealed by a large green garbage bin.

There. That should at least be good enough for the night.

I lift my bag out of the car and hoof it through the rain and sleet to the motel. My sneakers squish into a puddle and after about thirty seconds, I'm drenched. I regret not parking closer, but I wouldn't have been able to sleep at night if my car were in plain sight.

The front door of the Baxter motel is made of rotting wood that's dark with moisture. There's also a screen door loosely attached to the hinges that smacks me in the shoulder before I shove it out of the way. The knob feels ice cold to touch, and it sticks when I try to turn it. But after a second, it gives way and then I'm inside.

The inside of the motel isn't much warmer than outside, but at least it's dry. Well, mostly. There's water dripping from the ceiling, leaving a small puddle next to me. A splintered wooden counter is in the back of the room, but nobody's behind it. A single lightbulb hangs from the ceiling, and as I stand there, the light flickers.

"Hello?" I call out.

No answer.

I take a few steps forward. All I can hear is the dripping of the water coming from the ceiling. The motel feels empty, but the lights are on. And I saw that light on upstairs as well.

"Hello?" I say again, louder this time.

Still no answer. This place is making me uneasy. I wanted to find something out of the way, but this is a bit more isolated than I expected. Then again, the thought of having to run through the freezing rain back to my car isn't too appealing.

"I'm here! Don't leave! I'm coming!"

I whip my head around at the voice from behind me. A few seconds later, a man emerges from a back room, carrying a mop and a bucket. He smiles at me, revealing a slightly crooked left incisor. "Hey," he says. "Sorry. I was in the back."

"No worries." I try to return his smile, but I'm too tired to put in the effort anymore.

He shifts the handle of the mop to his other hand. "So are you looking for a jump for your car or…?"

"Oh… no, I…" I look down at the bag that I had dropped beside me. "I was hoping to get a room for the night."

He blinks at me, as if such a thing had never occurred to him. "You want a *room*?"

I frown. "Sorry, I thought this was a motel…"

"It is." He scratches at his hair, which is the color of damp sand. He's maybe mid-thirties and good-looking, but not in the same way as Derek used to be. Derek was lead actor kind of handsome, whereas this guy would get more of a supporting role. But he seems nice. Harmless. Like he wouldn't hurt a fly. "We just don't usually get many... But yes, we've got a room available. No problem."

"Thanks," I say.

"Can you just..." He gestures over at the puddle of water on the floor. "I want to get this cleaned up before the floor gets damaged. Or *more* damaged." He shakes his head. "Every time it rains, it starts leaking."

My eyes stray up to the dark spot on the ceiling where the drops of water are coalescing. "But isn't there another level above this one?"

He gives me a lopsided grin. "Right. It's a mystery."

He carries the bucket over to the puddle on the floor, then he dips the mop in the water. The puddle shrinks.

"Do you own this place?" I ask.

He nods. "Me and my wife do, yes."

As he pushes the mop across the floor, I noticed the glint of a wedding band on his left hand. I look down at my own left hand and see the simple gold band still in place. All of a sudden, it feels like it's burning my skin. I want to rip it off and throw it across the room.

"I'm Nick, by the way," he says.

"Hi, Nick," I say, but I don't offer my own name. He doesn't seem bothered by it.

Nick gives the mop one last shove across the floor, then rests it against the wall. He places the bucket in the place where the water is dripping down. I suppose that's his makeshift solution.

Once he's taken care of that, he goes behind the wooden counter. He leans his elbows on the counter as he looks at me. "So usually we charge fifty dollars a night. Is that okay?"

"Is cash all right?"

"But of course." He rifles below the counter. "Are you planning to stay just for the night or longer?"

"Just the one night." And maybe not even that long. "Am I the only person staying here?"

He hesitates. "No. We have another guest. But she's more… long term."

He doesn't explain what that means, which is fine. I just want to feel like I'm not the only person in this semi-deserted motel. Yes, this guy *seems* harmless, but this is how scary campfire stories start. "What about you and your wife? Do you stay here?"

Nick shakes his head. "Nah. We live in that old house right behind the motel. But I'll stick around for a while in case you need anything. I've got to fix that leak, anyway."

He finally finds what he was looking for under the desk. It's a sheet of paper, old enough that it's turned stiff and yellow. It looks like some sort of information form for guests. He blows a layer of dust from the paper. "Would you fill this out for me?"

"Um, sure."

I pick up the ballpoint pen on the desk, but my hand feels frozen. I don't want to fill this out. I'll have to falsify every piece of information here. Starting with my name.

At some point, I'll have to shell out the money for a fake ID. But in the meantime, I should have a fake name to give people. Except *what*? It should be something common that rolls off the tongue. Nothing memorable.

Mary? Jennifer? Carol? My best friend in college was Kelly. That's innocuous enough. So I scribble down the name Kelly.

And now I need to think of a last name.

"I have to tell you," Nick says. "This is the longest anyone has ever taken to write their name."

My cheeks burn. "Oh…"

"Listen…" He reaches for the yellowing piece of paper. "Don't worry about the form. You're just staying for the night." He looks down at the one piece of information I gave him. "Okay, Kelly?"

"Okay," I say gratefully.

I reach into my purse and extract fifty dollars to pay him for the room. He takes the money and shoves it into the pocket of his jeans. Then he grabs a set of keys from under the counter.

"I'll show you the room," he says. He glances at my luggage. "Let me get your bag for you."

I start to protest, but what the hell? I'm exhausted, and he looks strong. May as well let him carry my bag.

I follow him up a set of stairs to the second floor. The stairs aren't lit at all, and with every step, they groan like the whole staircase is about to collapse at any second. I grab onto the banister for support, in case the stairs really do collapse, and it immediately shifts under my weight. This whole motel feels like it's about to fall apart any second now.

Nick notices and flashes me an apologetic smile. "I need to tighten a few of the screws. Sorry about that."

"No problem."

The entire second floor seems to be lit by a single lightbulb. There are three doors, two on the left and one on the right. Nick takes me past rooms 201 and 202, and then we stop at 203. He fishes the keys out of his pocket.

As he's getting the door open, I noticed the door to room 202 has cracked open. I turn around, and I feel rather than see somebody watching me from within the room. I tilt my head, trying to get a better look, but then the door slams closed.

"Is… is there somebody staying in room 202?" I ask.

Nick glances at 202, then back down at the keys. "Yeah. That's just Greta. She sort of… lives here. She won't bother you."

I can't shake this uneasy feeling that I should leave this motel right now. Grab my bag and get back on the road, no matter how hard it's raining or snowing. This place is trouble.

But that's silly. It's warm and dry in here. And there's an actual bed that I can sleep in.

Nick throws open the door to my room for the night. It's about what I expected. A small double bed with a stiff looking bedspread, and an old dresser with a small TV balanced on top. And a rickety wooden chair in the corner of the room.

A crease forms between Nick's eyebrows as he watches my face. "Is it okay?"

"It's perfect," I say.

He nods. "The TV has an antenna… It's not cable or anything. We might get a little reception, but I'm not sure if you will in the storm. And there's a phone… But it only calls the phones on the first floor. Most people have cell phones these days…"

I think about the cell phone I tossed in the back of that pickup truck. I wish more than anything that I had a phone right now. But it's better I got rid of it. I don't want anyone to track me here. Plus, if I could call Claudia, I'm not sure if I could resist the temptation.

"And there's a private bathroom," he adds, a touch proudly. "So you can… You don't have to leave the room or anything. There's a shower and everything."

I shiver. "I don't shower at motels. When I was a kid, I saw this movie where this woman got murdered while taking a shower at a motel. It scarred me for life."

He smiles. "Well, it's there if you change your mind. I

promise you won't be murdered."

To be honest, I'm tempted. My hair is damp and freezing—a hot shower seems like heaven right now.

As I glance around the room, my stomach lets out a low growl. All I've eaten since lunch is those cheese doodles and a few Oreos while I was driving. And I have to say, I'm pretty burned out on cheese doodles and Oreos right now.

"Is there a way to get food?" I ask.

Nick chews his lower lip. "Uh… sure. We don't have room service or anything, but I could throw something together for you in our kitchen. Like… a turkey sandwich?"

"That sounds amazing," I breathe.

He laughs. "Oh, it won't be. Believe me. My wife, Rosalie, she was the cook."

I freeze for a moment. Did he just refer to his wife in the past tense? That's odd. And the name Rosalie sounds strangely familiar.

Then it hits me where I heard the name before. The restaurant next to the motel. The one that's all boarded up, where I parked my car. It was called Rosalie's.

"Anyway," he says, "make yourself comfortable. I'll go make that turkey sandwich. If there's anything you need, just dial zero on the telephone and it will ring downstairs. I'm going to be sticking around for a while fixing things."

"Thanks," I say.

He flashes me a disarming smile, and my shoulders relax. My first impression was right. Nick is a nice guy. I'm safe here, at least for the night, but first thing in the morning, I've got to get the hell out of here.

CHAPTER 8

After Nick leaves, I watch him walk down the hall, then back down those creaky stairs. When I swivel my head, the door to room 202 is cracked open again.

And this time, there's a single eye staring out at me.

I raise my hand in a tentative greeting, but before I can even get it in the air, the door swings shut again. Okay then.

I take a cue from my neighbor and shut my door behind me. I turn the lock, then notice the deadbolt on top. I hesitate for a moment, then throw that as well. Not that I think anybody is going to murder me in the shower, but better not to take chances.

My shirt and pants stayed relatively dry under my coat, but my socks and sneakers are absolutely soaked. I kick off my sneakers and then peel my socks off my feet. Fortunately, there's a radiator in the room, next to the window, so I put my wet sneakers and socks on top of it.

The view from the window overlooks a small, two-story house a stone's throw away that looks as badly in need of repair as the motel itself. It's hard to see with the ice coming down, but light is on in one of the second-story windows. There's the outline of a woman sitting in the window. That must be Rosalie, Nick's wife. I awkwardly raise my hand to wave to her.

She doesn't wave back. People don't seem terribly friendly here. And that's just fine.

I step away from the window and open up my luggage. It takes me less than a minute to realize the horrible truth. I forgot to pack *socks*. I brought my jewelry, but I didn't bring socks. If Claudia were here, she would tease me mercilessly. And I would deserve it, because who goes on the run without bringing a few pairs of socks with them?

God, I miss Claudia so much. It's a good thing the phone doesn't dial outside lines, because I would be painfully tempted to call her. And that would be a terrible idea, even though I'm desperate to hear her voice just one last time. If she were with me, I would have known to pack socks.

If I had listened to her in the first place, I never would have married Derek.

She warned me. *Repeatedly*. She told me she didn't think he was a good guy. But he was just so perfect when he was courting me. There was no way to know what kind of monster he was.

But up until today, I didn't know quite how awful he

was.

Some of our senior staff had to go to a conference this weekend, so they all took off early. The bank closed shortly after lunch, and we were given an unexpected half-day. I was excited to have an afternoon off. I rarely had the house to myself, and I thought I could take a nice long shower, then watch television as loud as I wanted without Derek yelling at me to keep it down.

But then when I walked through the front door, Derek was already home. I was shocked to see him. And he seemed even more shocked to see me. The second I entered the living room, his face contorted in anger.

What are you doing here? he demanded to know.

Nothing, I stammered. *I got out of work early, that's all.*

Are you sure that's all you're here for? Or are you meeting some guy?

I tried to explain about the conference. The unexpected half day. I plastered a smile on my face and tried to suggest we do something together, as a couple. Maybe go to the movies or go shopping. Or up to the bedroom, even.

But Derek couldn't let it go. He kept insisting I came home to meet another man. And the jealousy was ironic, given I was certain he had cheated on me many times. He even kept an apartment in Boston, which he claimed was for business purposes since his company is based in the city, but I'm pretty sure it was his little bachelor pad.

I tried to talk him down, but it became obvious he was working himself into a rage. I had never seen him quite like this. But even when his hands balled into fists, I didn't really think he was going to hurt me until I felt his hands around my neck.

And that was the last straw. He pushed me around long enough. I would not let him take my life.

The part that I still don't understand is why he got so angry this time. For a moment, when I first came home, he had been smiling. I thought he was having a good day. I thought we might have a pleasant afternoon together. He seemed happy to see me, and then a second later, the smile dropped off his face. I don't understand why…

Oh my God.

It finally makes sense. Why he was smiling when he heard someone was at the door, then he immediately got angry. He was happy because *he didn't know it was me.* He was expecting somebody else.

Another woman.

I sink down onto the bed, shivering from my cold feet. It makes total sense. Derek came home early to meet some other woman. And when he saw me, he was angry because I had ruined his tryst by showing up. Also, in his warped mind, he assumed anyone coming home early was there to fool around, because that's what he was doing.

I feel sick. This is not good news. I can only hope that in the last minutes of his life, Derek sent a text message to his girlfriend to tell her not to come. Because if he didn't…

The police may have already discovered his body.

And if that's the case, it means they're already looking for me. And I have left them a wonderful trail of breadcrumbs. That gas station. The police officer who pulled me over for the broken tail light, for God's sake. And here I am, a sitting duck in a hotel only about twenty minutes from where I was last spotted.

But then again, there's a blizzard evolving outside. That will make it hard for them to search for me. And moreover, the blizzard makes it impossible for me to leave. Not tonight, anyway.

I grab the remote control from the end table and turn on the television. Immediately, snow fills the screen. That's right—this television has an antenna. I can't remember the last time I dealt with a television antenna. I have only vague memories of my parents fiddling with an antenna when I was barely out of diapers. I didn't know they even still made television antennas. But then again, this TV looks extremely old—like they bought it cheap at a pawn shop. Everything in this hotel looks like it was made several decades ago.

I get up out of bed and wince as my bare feet touch the freezing wooden floor. I walk over to the television and attempt to adjust the antenna. After a minute, I get a clear picture, although if I let go of the antenna, it fades away. So I guess I have to stand here if I want to watch television.

I don't want to watch television. I just want to see the news.

There's a pretty, blond woman on the screen, announcing the top stories for the night. Mostly, they're talking about the blizzard. I listen carefully, waiting to hear anything about the murder of a thirty-four-year-old man named Derek Alexander.

Nothing. Maybe I'm in the clear. At least for now.

I shiver again. My feet feel like blocks of ice. How could I forget to bring socks? Who would be that stupid? Then again, it's not like I was thinking clearly.

After a moment of consideration, I release the antenna, and the picture on the television turns to snow again. But that's fine. I pick up the phone and dial zero.

It rings about five times before I hear Nick's voice on the other line. "Kelly? Everything okay?"

My first thought is, *Who is Kelly?* Then I remember.

"Um…" I feel a little silly asking this. "I'm just wondering… Do you have any extra socks?"

He chuckles. "Well, no. Not here. I could ask my wife if…" He pauses. "You know what? You should ask Greta. In room 202. She'll give you some socks."

"Greta?" Given that she slammed the door in my face when I was about to wave to her, I'm reluctant to knock on her door and attempt to ask her for socks. "She doesn't seem very friendly."

"No, she's just… She's nice. Really. She's an old

woman. Harmless."

"I don't know…" My eyes dart over to the radiator, where my socks still look sopping wet. If anything, they look even *more* wet than when I put them there. "I guess I could ask…"

"She'll be happy to give you some socks. She's a little eccentric, but she's just lonely. But I promise, she's nice. She's lived here for years."

I'm not excited about this, but Nick doesn't seem like he's going to rustle up a pair of socks for me. So if I want my feet to be warm and dry, this is my only option. "Okay."

"And I'll be up in a few minutes with the turkey sandwich. Sorry… I got a bit… delayed."

After we hang up the phone, I stare at the door to the room. Nick said the woman in 202 is a harmless old lady, but there was something about those eyes staring out at me from the crack in her door. It creeped me out. And if the police do eventually show up here looking for me, I don't need another witness they can talk to.

Then again, my feet are freezing.

To hell with it. I flip open the deadlock and unlock the door, then I tromp across the hallway in my bare feet to room 202. I hesitate for half a second, then knock on the door.

After a good ten seconds, I hear a voice behind the door. "Who is it?"

"Um, hi." I chew on my thumbnail—a bad habit I had

as a child that seems to have resurfaced. "I'm staying in room 203. Across the hall. And... I was wondering if you could help me out with something."

There's a long silence. For a moment, I wonder if she simply walked away. But then I hear the turning of locks, and a second later, the door cracks open.

For the first time, I can see her clearly. She's older than I thought. Her hair is long and fine, and as white as the snow falling outside. Every millimeter of her face is lined with wrinkles. Her watery blue eyes stare up at me.

"What do you need?" she says in a crackly voice. She sounds like she used to be a smoker. Or maybe she still is, but I don't smell cigarette smoke coming from her room.

I smile apologetically. "Socks, actually. I forgot to pack them for my trip."

Her eyes drop to my bare feet. Then back up again to my face. "You want to borrow a pair of socks?"

"Yes." I squeeze my hands together. "I'll rinse them out in the morning when my own socks are dry."

"If you are going on a trip, it is important to pack socks."

"Right. I know. I just forgot."

She considers this for a moment. Finally, she backs away from the door and opens it enough to allow me inside.

Room 202 looks a lot different from my room. It's about the same size, maybe slightly larger, but it looks lived in. Nick told me she has been staying in this room for years, and I believe it. Instead of the stiff bedspread in my own room, her blankets are made of wool and covered with exotic multicolored patterns. She has multiple lamps that give the room a yellow glow. And the wall is lined with mirrors, so I can see myself no matter where I look.

I don't look too good right now.

"I am Greta," she says. She has the very slightest hint of an accent that I can't identify. East European, I think.

"I'm Kelly," I say.

She sniffs. "If you do not want to give me a real name, don't even bother."

I open my mouth to protest, but then shut it. She's right. That isn't my real name.

As I wait for Greta to rifle around inside her dresser drawer, I look down at a deck of cards she has on her dresser. It takes me a second to realize that they're not playing cards, but rather Tarot cards. Next to them is an orb that glows in the yellow light of the room.

Greta sees me noticing them and comments, "I was a fortune teller at a carnival for thirty years."

I manage a smile. "So you can read the future?"

She pauses for a moment and looks up at me. Her watery blue eyes rake over my bedraggled appearance. "For some, yes."

I don't really believe in any of that stuff, but I don't tell her that. It seems like she's getting a kick out of trying to freak me out. As long as I get my socks.

"I have stockings," she finally says, as she pulls a pair of crinkled tan stockings from the drawer. "Is it socks you require?"

"Well, I don't *require* them." I shift between my feet. "But if you have them…"

Greta holds up a finger. She throws open the closet on the wall and pulls out a large black trunk that probably weighs more than she does. She fiddles with the lock to get it open. I feel guilty that she's going to so much trouble for a pair of socks.

"Have you lived here a long time?" I ask politely.

"Many years," she confirms. "Since I retired." She raises her eyes. "You are in room 203."

"That's right," I say. "And I guess 201 is empty then."

The lock on the trunk opens with a click. "Nick always leaves 201 empty."

I nod. "Because of the leaky pipe, right?"

"No," she says. "Not because of that."

"Then… why?"

"Because…" Greta pulls a ball of socks out of the trunk and gets back on her feet while holding onto the wall for support. "Because a couple of years ago, a woman was murdered in there."

She says it so matter-of-factly, like this is something everyone must know. That somebody was killed here in the recent past.

Yet again, I desperately wish I had my phone. I could

find out in a second what went down at the Baxter Motel. I have a feeling Greta here knows all the details.

"What happened?" I ask.

Greta clutches the sock ball in her hand, studying my face with her shrewd eyes. "It was a pretty young woman, like you. About your age. Also with blond hair. Her name was Christina Marsh. She came to stay here for a few days, but then I noticed she hadn't come out of her room in a while." She looks over my shoulder, at something in the distance. "It wasn't just that though. Something was wrong. I knew it. So I told Nick to go check on her. And…"

I stare at her, not wanting to hear the rest of the story. But unable to keep from hearing it.

"She was lying in her bed, stabbed to death," she says. "Nick found her there. The police said she'd been dead for about a day."

I clasp my hand over my mouth. "That's horrible. Did they ever find out who did it?"

She shakes her head slowly. "They never did, but they suspected Nick. There were no signs of forced entry, so it stood to reason whoever killed her had access to her room."

"Oh." I remember my first impression of Nick, and how I thought he was the sort of person who wouldn't hurt a fly. But impressions aren't always right. "Do you think that he…?"

Greta is silent for a moment. She stares up at me with those watery, red-veined eyes.

"No," she says. "Nick would never do something like that. The police had it wrong. I told them as much."

I let out a breath and my shoulders sag. I don't know what I would have done if Greta told me she thought Nick was a murderer. But of course she wouldn't think that. Why would she live here if she thought the owner was a killer?

"But there was another reason they thought Nick killed her," she adds.

I raise my eyebrows. "What reason?"

Her slightly yellow tongue protrudes from her mouth and she licks her lips. "I don't like to tell tales."

Really? Because it seems to me she likes to tell tales very much. But I can't say that.

She holds the socks out to me, and I take them. The material feels rough in my hands, like they haven't been worn in decades. But they will do.

"Thank you," I say.

She nods. "Be careful."

I don't know what she means by that. She's not wrong—I am in danger. But she doesn't know why.

As I turn, I come face-to-face with yet another mirror. Why does she have so many mirrors in her room? It's hard to look at myself right now. My blond hair is limp and lifeless, and so short now that I don't even recognize myself. My eyes look sunken in their sockets, and my cheeks are dark as well. If anything looks frightening in this place, it's me.

"I love mirrors," Greta tells me. "Mirrors are the barrier between the conscious and unconscious mind. Everyone has an inner concept of themselves, but mirrors are reality. What you see right now—that is the truth that everyone else sees."

"Right," I mumble.

"If you stay here," she says, "I'll do a reading for you tomorrow. You may find it enlightening."

"That's okay. I'm not staying."

"The future may surprise you."

If I wasn't feeling so uneasy, I might have rolled my eyes. This woman can't see into the future. She doesn't even have socks in her drawer. She's obviously trying to scare me. I bet nobody even died in room 201. She probably made the whole thing up to freak me out.

Well, it won't work.

"Thanks for the socks," I say. "I'll leave them on your doorstep in the morning."

"Keep them," she says. "You should have an extra pair of socks." `

It's a nice gesture, although the second I make it out of here, I'm going to buy some socks in a drugstore or something. And some hair dye.

I slip out of her room, the socks clutched in my right hand. I can't see the future but I predict I will never see this woman again.

CHAPTER 9

The socks are horrific.

I suppose I shouldn't be surprised, considering what that woman's room looked like. They are just as stiff and uncomfortable as I thought they would be, but the worst part is the pattern on them. At first, I think it's just diamonds and ovals. But after a second, I realize what it actually is. Eyes.

The pattern on the socks is eyes.

Just as I get the eyeball socks on, I hear a knock at the door. I nearly fling it open, but then I remember Greta's story about the woman who was murdered in her room. "Yes?"

"It's Nick. I've got a turkey sandwich for you."

Just as he says the words, my stomach lets out a growl. I had almost forgotten how hungry I was. I unlock the door, and Nick is standing there with a white plate in his hand.

"Thank you!" I take the plate from him and without even putting it down, I grab half of the sandwich and start stuffing it in my mouth. *Mmm...*

He laughs at my eagerness. "Good?"

"Yeah, so good. Sorry I'm being rude."

"Not at all." He grins. "I'm just glad you like it. It's just, you know, whatever we had in the fridge."

I stuff another bite into my mouth. "What do I owe you?"

He shakes his head. "Don't worry about it. Meals are included."

"Oh. Okay." I feel a little bad about it, considering he doesn't have many guests, and it looks like this place is falling apart, so I'm thinking he's not rolling in it. But then again, I'm not in any position to be throwing around money. "Thank you again."

He glances down at my feet. "I see you got your socks. Greta gave them to you?"

"Yes, she did. She's, um, very interesting..."

Nick throws back his head and laughs. "Yeah, she is, isn't she? Did she offer to tell your fortune?"

Despite myself, I laugh too. "Yes, she did."

"That's her thing. She was some sort of carnival psychic. It's all a good show."

I pause before taking another bite of my turkey sandwich. "Did she ever tell your fortune?"

He snorts. "Yeah. She told me the usual thing. You're going to die young. Horrible misfortune. Like I said, it's a good show—it's what she does. I wish she could've told me about that pipe breaking. Now *that* would've been useful."

I swallow a chunk of turkey and bread. "Did a woman really die in room 201?"

The smile vanishes from Nick's face. Whatever else, it's obvious this particular piece of information is absolutely true. "She told you that?"

I nod.

He rubs at the back of his neck. "What did she say?"

I study his face. His light brown eyes. The stubble on his chin. "She said it was a young woman, and she was stabbed to death in the room. And you found her."

He coughs. "Um, yeah. All of that is true."

A chill goes down my spine and then all the way to my toes, even though I'm wearing socks now. "That must've been awful."

"Yeah." His eyes drop. "It was. I've never seen anything like that before. I never want to see it again. I still sometimes have nightmares."

"That's horrible," I murmur. "And they never found out who killed her?"

He lifts his eyes. But he's not looking at me. He's looking at the window behind me. "No. They never did."

"Oh," I murmur.

"Anyway." His smile seems forced. "If there isn't

anything else you need, I'm going to head back over to my house. Rosalie... She doesn't like to be alone when there's a storm. I can fix the pipe in the morning."

"Of course." I think of the silhouette in the window of the house across the way. The woman who didn't wave back. "Will your wife be over here in the morning?"

Nick shakes his head. "No. She doesn't come to the motel anymore. She's been... ill. I've been taking care of her."

"Oh gosh, I'm so sorry. That must be hard."

He lifts a shoulder. "She's my wife. In sickness and in health, right?" He looks pointedly at the wedding band on my left hand. "You know what I'm talking about."

I suck in a breath. I can't tell him I just stuck a knife in the man who gave me this ring. "Yes. Of course."

"Good night, Kelly. I'll see you in the morning."

I clutch the plate with my half-finished turkey sandwich while I watch Nick walk down the hall. He seemed like he was in such a good mood until I brought up the murder in 201. He's obviously still very affected by it.

There was another reason they thought Nick killed her.

Everything Greta told me in that room was true. I wonder what she was talking about that time.

Anyway, it doesn't matter. I won't be in this motel for much longer. First thing in the morning, I'm back on the road. As soon as the snow stops.

I flip around the "DO NOT DISTURB" sign on my

door, then I close the door and lock it. I walk over to the window, watching the flakes fall from the sky. I wish I could check the weather app on my phone to see how long this is going on for. I should've checked it out before I ditched my phone. I've got a shovel in the back of my car though. I'm getting out of here, one way or another.

I look across the way, at the small house right next door. It's run down, but there's something majestic about the large, swooping windows, the brick chimney, and the cone jutting from the top floor—almost like it's a castle. With some work, it could be really beautiful. It's a fixer-upper, that's for sure. Nick said his wife was sick—I wonder if they had plans to fix it all up, but then got derailed.

I know what it's like to have plans get derailed.

That light is still on in the upstairs window. The silhouette of Rosalie Baxter stares right back at me. I don't lift my hand this time. In fact, I let the curtains fall closed, with only a small crack between them.

That's when I see movement behind Rosalie's silhouette. It must be Nick, having come home. I peer through the tiny crack in the curtains, watching them. He bends down next to her, talking to her. He reaches out and touches her face. I expect him to lean in to kiss her, but he doesn't.

I watch as he stands up. Suddenly, he's pacing the room. He seems upset, but of course, I can't hear a word of the conversation.

And then he stops pacing. He lifts his head and looks straight through the window.

I jerk my head away from the window. He couldn't possibly see me, could he? No, it's impossible. But either way, I shouldn't be snooping. Whatever he's doing with his wife in his own home is private. It's none of my business.

I turn back to the television. I'm dying to know if there's anything on the news about Derek. There's no way for me to leave this motel tonight, but if they haven't discovered the body yet, I have a bit of breathing room. I really wish I had my phone with me to browse the web, but that would've made me a sitting duck.

I turn on the television, but the entire screen is just a mass of snow. I fiddle with the antenna, turning it every which way, making it longer, then shorter. It's hopeless—there's no reception. It's probably because of the storm.

Well, maybe if the storm is this bad, it means they're not out there looking for me.

I wince at the thought of Scott Dwyer discovering my husband's dead body. I still don't quite understand why he didn't insist on coming into the house to check things out. Isn't that protocol? If you hear screams, don't you have to look inside?

But he's going to find the body eventually. I wish it could be somebody else who makes the discovery. I don't want Scott to know what a mess my life has become in the last decade.

A sob rises up at the bottom of my throat when I think back to the simpler days in high school, when I first got to know Scott. Of course, my life was far from perfect then. The pain of both my parents being suddenly killed was still raw. Most days, I went straight home after school and studied. Before my parents died, I used to get involved in extracurricular activities, but I couldn't bring myself to do it anymore. Especially since they had been going to see one of my plays when the accident happened.

For most of high school, I kept to myself. I kept my nose in a book, and most of the other kids saw me as aloof or even stuck up. Anyway, they left me alone.

But Scott made an effort. He would talk to me in class, and he started walking me to my next class afterwards. He would joke around until I would smile, which was no small feat because I did not smile easily. Then one day, while we were talking about how unseasonably hot it was outside, I noticed his shoulder brushing against mine as we walked. He noticed too, and he grinned in my direction. Whenever he looked at me, it was with this expression of unbridled affection. Like he thought I was the coolest, most wonderful girl he'd ever met.

And then when we got to my social studies class (he had a class at the exact same time at the entire other end of the school, and was undoubtedly late for it every single day because of me), he rubbed a hand through his hair, enough to make it stick up straight in the air. His smile was adorably nervous.

It's so hot outside. Maybe we could go to Frosty's for some ice cream after class is over?

It took me a split second to realize what was happening. Scott was asking me out on a date. And I realized how much I wanted it. *That sounds nice.*

I didn't appreciate him. I was too young, and I didn't know what other boys were like. I thought every boy would race around the side of his broken down Ford to keep me from opening the door on my own. Would drive me home every single day after school, even if it meant he had to rush back to school to get to swim team practice. Would kiss me softly and sweetly and respectfully ask permission before he tried anything we hadn't done before.

Unlike Derek, who always had some idea of perfection I could never achieve, Scott seemed thrilled just to be with me.

He was sweet, yes. But also a bit boring. A bit too nice. And I was going to college, while he was sticking around our hometown, working at his dad's store. It seemed very much like a high school kind of relationship, and I never really thought we would stay together when I went to college. And we didn't.

Then when I moved back to the town after college, I ran into him at the grocery store and found out he had become a police officer. And also that he had filled out quite nicely. And the way he was looking at me, I could tell he still felt the same way about me that he did in high school.

Maybe we could get a drink later? he suggested.

But I had just started my job at the bank, and I was so busy trying to make a good impression. So I put him off, thinking we would do it another time, and then that other time never came. And then of course, Derek entered my life.

I imagine Scott walking into the kitchen at my old house, the one I'll probably never see again. I imagine him looking down at Derek's dead body, his eyes filling with disgust. The next time I see Scott, he won't give me that familiar look of affection.

He'll never look at me that way again.

God, I have made such a mess of everything.

I push thoughts of Scott Dwyer out of my head. Right now, I need to sleep. I've got a long day of driving ahead of me, and since there's nothing else I can do right now, I should do my best to rest up.

But I have a bad feeling sleep will be difficult.

CHAPTER 10

I got the worst night's sleep of my life.

I didn't lie awake. That would have been preferable to what happened, which is that I dozed off and woke up every hour on the hour with horrible nightmares. But they weren't exactly nightmares. They were memories.

We had our first date at a French restaurant. It was so much fancier than what I was used to. We didn't have a lot of money growing up, and of course, things got much harder after our parents died and it was just me and Claudia. I wasn't used to being spoiled that way.

I opened up the menu and was immediately intimidated. It was entirely in French, and I had a feeling that even if I spoke French, I wouldn't have known what half these dishes were. I timidly asked Derek what was good, and he told me he would order for both of us. He didn't even ask me what sort of things I liked to eat, but his confidence was compelling. It was so different from every other man I'd ever dated.

Derek ordered some special fancy red wine. He actually sniffed the cork. The server poured it into my glass, and Derek watched eagerly as I took a sip. *What do you think, Quinn?*

I sat there, unsure how to distinguish this fancy wine from the kind I got for ten dollars from the local liquor store. *It's got a fruity note,* I finally said. (It didn't. It tasted *exactly* like the ten dollar wine.)

Derek beamed at me, and I felt like I had gotten the right answer on a test. He was so handsome and dripping with charm and charisma. He seemed *better* than me. Claudia would have been angry if I said that, but I couldn't help feeling that way.

He ordered us something called coq au vin, which he explained was hen braised in red wine. I also tried foie gras, which is apparently duck liver. It tasted terrible to me, but over the last several years, I grew to appreciate the taste.

And then as we were finishing up the most divine chocolate soufflé, Derek leaned in and kissed me.

In real life, it was a lovely kiss that led to a second date, then a third, then far too soon, a proposal I couldn't say no to. But in my dream, we had that same dinner, the same expensive wine, and the same delicious chocolate soufflé. And he kissed me the same way. But then when he pulled away, there was a red stain spreading across his white dress shirt.

Quinn, he gasped.

I looked down and saw a steak knife in my right hand. It was covered in my husband's blood. I let it clatter to the floor, but it was too late.

You bitch, Derek managed as the color drained from his face. *Call... an ambulance...*

But I didn't call an ambulance. I just stood there, watching the life drain out of him.

I let my husband die on the floor of my kitchen.

So that's my other secret. I stabbed Derek in the abdomen to keep him from strangling me, but there was a moment when I might have been able to save him. If I had run straight to the phone and called 911, maybe he would be alive right now. But I didn't. Yes, I killed him in self-defense, but I wanted him to die.

Not only that, but I waited to make sure he was dead. I stood there, watching him bleed out. As he cried for help. He begged me to call an ambulance until he lost consciousness. And even after he was unconscious, I still waited. Waited until his chest stopped rising and falling. Waited until I couldn't feel a pulse in his wrist.

I wake up with a start in my uncomfortable double bed in the hotel room. For a moment, I'm completely disoriented. I have no idea where I am. But then it all comes rushing back to me. Where I am. What I've done.

I sit up in bed, my heart pounding.

I've got to get out of here.

I look at my wrist watch—it's close to nine o'clock. I don't know how I managed to sleep so late when I was hardly sleeping at all. But I can't even waste a second getting back on the road. I don't have time to attempt to get the television to work to check out the news. I'll listen to it on the car radio.

I hit the bathroom to empty my bladder and splash some water on my face. When I look at my reflection in the mirror, I flinch. I look awful. My blond hair is at least dry by now, but it looks like it was cut with... well, with a pair of scissors in somebody's bathroom. The strands are limp and lifeless, and there are dark purple circles under my eyes. I look like I've aged ten years overnight.

But the worst part is I still look like me. Yes, a bedraggled version of me, but I'm still clearly Quinn Alexander. If anybody saw a photograph of me, I'm recognizable, even with my hair hacked off.

I don't know what to do to change my appearance. In the short term, I need to buy some hair dye. Something dark, but not a black color that will draw attention. And I can try to pack on some weight, although I can't imagine how I'll accomplish that when I have no money for food.

Anyway, I'll figure it out later. Right now, I've got to get out of here.

As I pull on my blue jeans, I hear a rap at the door. My

heart thuds in my chest. Is it the police? Have they come looking for me? But then I hear Nick's voice.

"Kelly?"

"Hang on!" I grab my socks off the radiator. They're very stiff, but warm and dry. I stuff my feet into them and run a hand through my hacked off hair. "Coming!"

I crack open the door, and Nick is standing there, holding a plate of food. It appears to be scrambled eggs and a few slices of crisp bacon. My stomach growls at the sight of it.

"Sorry to disturb you…" He looks pointedly at the sign hung from my doorknob. "But I made you some breakfast. I figured you'd be hungry."

He's right. At the sight of the plate of food, my stomach groans painfully. The eggs are brown, but I couldn't care less. I could devour them in one bite. "Thanks. I'm going to get on the road pretty soon though."

Nick's eyebrows shoot up to his hairline. "On the road?"

"Yeah…" I glance out the window. "The snow stopped, right?"

"Right, but…" He frowns. "We're buried. I can't get a plow to come out here till the late afternoon. I don't see where you parked, but unless you've got a huge truck, I don't see how you're getting out of here."

My stomach sinks. "Are you serious?"

He shifts between his feet. "I'm sorry. I can try calling

the plow company again. But we got about two feet of snow here last night..."

No, no, no... this can't be happening. I've got to get out of here. "Maybe I could dig out my car."

"Uh..."

I grip the white plate in my hands, my appetite suddenly gone. "Would you help me?"

"Help you?"

"Help dig me out." I'm gripping the plate so hard, it feels like it might shatter in my hands. "I've got to get out of here today. Please."

"Uh..." Nick glances over my shoulder, out the window at the blinding white snow coating absolutely everything. "I guess we can try, but there's a lot of snow out there. Where did you park anyway? You're not in the lot right outside."

"I parked by that diner. The one that's boarded up."

"Okay." He lifts his shoulders. "We can give it a shot." He looks down at my feet. "You got boots?"

Of course I don't have boots. I didn't even have freaking socks. "No. It's fine though."

He rubs the stubble on his jaw. "Let me borrow a pair from Rosalie. You look like you're about the same size."

Something about borrowing a pair of boots from his sick wife makes me feel a little uneasy. "It's fine."

"It's *not* fine. There's a *lot* of snow out there. You're going to lose a toe if you don't have a pair of decent boots on."

He makes a good point. "If you're sure it's okay…"

He nods at the plate of food. "Why don't you eat breakfast, then I'll meet you downstairs with the boots."

I agree to do it, but his expression doesn't make me feel hopeful. What if I can't get out of here? I'm a sitting duck right now.

After he's gone, I shovel eggs into my mouth while I attempt to get reception on the television. The eggs are pretty terrible. They are dry and bland, and the bacon is burned. He did better with the turkey sandwich. To be fair, it's hard to ruin a turkey sandwich.

I tune into the local news, but there's no mention of any sort of murder. Again, most of the news is about the blizzard. I don't know if it's just that the story hasn't hit the news yet, or if nobody has discovered Derek's body yet.

It seems almost impossible they haven't discovered him yet. That he's just lying on the kitchen floor, dead, and nobody knows it. How long does it take for a body to decompose? It couldn't already be happening, could it? Not in the cold, at least.

It's almost impossible to think of Derek that way. He was so strong and big and full of life. He was larger than life. For him to be dead…

He *is* dead, isn't he?

Isn't he?

The thought hadn't occurred to me. I stood there and

waited to make sure he was gone. He bled out all over the kitchen floor. He's definitely dead. He wasn't breathing.

He's *dead*.

But…

It's not like I'm a doctor. It *seemed* like he wasn't breathing. I couldn't feel a pulse. He was so still. And there was *so* much blood. There's no way he could still be alive.

Before I left the house, I didn't check him. I couldn't bear to. I just assumed he was still lying on the kitchen floor, the way I left him. It's like that feeling you get when you left your house in the morning and you're not sure if you shut off the lights or locked the door. Except a million times worse.

What if the reason nobody's looking for me is that Derek isn't actually dead?

I feel like I'm going to throw up the eggs I just ate. A few moments ago, I felt confident of one thing: Derek was dead. I was sure of it. But now I'm not so sure anymore. What if he got up off the floor, got himself patched up, and now he's out there looking for me?

Either way, I need to get the hell out of here.

I look down at my left hand, where my wedding band is still there, taunting me. Whatever else, I want that stupid thing off my hand. I yank it off roughly. My skin is a couple of shades whiter where the band used to be. The first thing I'm going to do is get rid of that tan line.

I pull open the dresser drawer next to the bed. The only

thing inside is a copy of the Bible. I shove my ring in the drawer and slam it shut.

I grab the key to the room and lock it behind me when I leave. I consider bringing my bag with me, but I decide to leave it behind. I can swing by the motel entrance and toss it in on my way out.

"Leaving so soon?"

I whirl around—Greta standing behind me. She's wearing a long, light blue nightgown that grazes her ankles. Unlike me, she doesn't seem all bothered by being in her bare feet.

"Uh, yeah," I say. "Got to get going."

"There's a great deal of snow out there."

"Right," I say irritably. "Nick is going to help me dig my car out."

Greta looks down at my feet. All I've got on now are my socks. "Interesting choice of footwear."

I grit my teeth. "Nick told me he would borrow a pair of boots from his wife."

Greta's lips curl up. "Be careful what you borrow from that man's wife."

Something about her expression makes me very uneasy. "He said it was fine. It was his idea."

"Of course it was." She scoffs. "I'm just saying. Rosalie will not be happy about handing over a pair of her boots so that her husband can help a pretty young guest." Her eyes narrow at me. "She's always watching him, you know."

I think of the shadow in the window of the house across from the motel. My breath catches. "There's nothing to be jealous of. Believe me."

"Tell that to Christina Marsh."

My throat goes dry. What is she saying? Is she implying that Rosalie Baxter had something to do with the death of that girl in Room 201?

But no. That's crazy. Nick said that his wife is sick. She's ill—she's not going around murdering anyone.

Of course, he didn't say what she was sick with. What if she's mentally ill?

I shake my head. This is ridiculous. I'm going to be gone within the hour. I don't need to think about Nick's crazy wife. And Greta is just trying to scare me. Nick said she had a flair for the dramatic.

"It'll be fine," I say to Greta. "It was…. nice meeting you." Not really.

The expression on the old woman's face is unreadable. "Nice meeting you too… *Kelly*."

With those words, Greta slams the door in my face. I hear the locks clicking into place behind the door. Even though she and I are the only people here. And Nick, of course. I wonder why she feels she needs all those locks.

As I walk down the hall, I pass room 201. That's where it happened. That's where a girl was murdered two years ago.

I wonder what it must've been like to discover her.

Nick would have opened the door with his master key, then found her lying on the bedspread, the fabric stained with her blood. Surely, he had to throw out the bedspread. I know now how hard it is to get blood out.

I shiver. I don't need to think about this anymore. After today, I'm never going to see the Baxter Motel ever again.

As promised, Nick is waiting for me on the first floor. He's got on a heavy black coat and a black beanie on his head. When he grins at me, he looks sort of adorable. Derek was undeniably handsome, but I always preferred guys like Nick. Those boy-next-door good looks.

"Got you some boots!" He holds up a pair of black, fur-lined snow boots. "This will keep you warm."

"Thanks." I reach for the boots, but then I hesitate. "Are you sure it's okay if I borrow them?"

"Yeah!" He bobs his head. "Of course. She never wears them anymore anyway. You could probably just, you know, have them."

There's no way I am taking his wife's boots. But I'll wear them until I get my car free.

When I get outside the motel and see all the snow, I feel sick. Nick wasn't exaggerating. This looks like way more than two feet of snow. In some areas, it looks like ten feet of snow. And I'm driving a Corolla, not a pickup truck. How in the hell am I going to get out of here?

"Wow," I mumble. "I didn't realize how bad it was."

He nods. "What sort of car do you have?"

"A Corolla."

His eyes widen. "Well, this will be a challenge."

To his credit, he still seems game to help me. Rosalie's boots sink into the deep white powder as we make our way very slowly over to the diner where I parked my car. When I explain that we have to walk all the way around the restaurant to my parking spot, Nick seems a bit surprised, but he goes along with it without questioning me why I would do something like that. He's got a shovel, and I've got one in the trunk of my car. But with each step, I'm realizing how impossible this is going to be. We are going to need to shovel the length of a football field to get me out of here.

When we get around the side of the restaurant, Nick squints into the whiteness. "Where is your car? I don't see it."

I don't see it either. Shit, where did my car go?

But then I see the big mound of snow behind the dumpster, and I notice a little patch of the blue side mirror. That's my car. It's just been buried. I would have hoped the restaurant might shield it from some of the snow, but this seems more consistent with my luck recently.

"It's over there," I say.

Nick nods, and we made our way over to that immense pile of snow that buried my car last night. When we get there, he has to steady himself on the hood of my car. "Jesus, this is a lot of snow," he comments.

"Thanks for helping me," I say.

"Yeah," he breathes. "Well… let's get to it."

He helps me clear off the trunk so that I can pop it open and get my own shovel as well as the ice scraper—a crucial tool for any New England winter. And then the two of us get to work.

It's slow going. There is a *lot* of snow on my car. And surrounding my car. And surrounding the area surrounding my car. I'm seriously discouraged, but Nick doesn't complain. He just keeps shoveling snow around my car.

"Thanks for your help," I say. "Really. I appreciate it so much."

He flashes me a smile. "No problem. Happy to help."

"I'm sure most owners of motels don't help their guests shovel snow."

He laughs. "Well, we're a full-service motel." He blinks up at me. "And if you need to stay longer, you're welcome to. We can, you know, work out a discount rate or something."

He's figured out money is tight for me. But the reason I'm not staying has nothing to do with the money. And anyway, from the looks of his crumbling motel, he's in no position to be offering anyone a discount. "Thanks," I mumble.

"And the food won't be any better," he continues cheerfully, "but at least there's plenty of it. Like that joke about the restaurant where the customers complain the food is so terrible? And then they say, 'And the portions are so small!'"

When I don't crack a smile, he adds, "You know, because why would you want a big portion if the food is terrible, right?"

I nod. "Yeah…"

He clears his throat. "Sorry, I'm just trying to get you to cheer up. I don't think I told that joke very well."

I manage a very tiny smile, just for his sake. I'm not feeling it though. "Don't worry about it. Whatever food you give me is fine."

"Like I said, my wife was the cook." Again, he's talking about her in the past tense. "It's just hard for her now."

Despite the cold, I wipe some sweat off my brow. Shoveling is hard work. On top of everything else, I'm going to be sore in all my muscles tomorrow. "So… this was her restaurant?"

Nick glances behind him at the boarded up building. "Yeah, it was. That was always her dream. To have her own restaurant. And for a while, it was doing really well. Really *really* well, considering it's just a tiny rest stop on the side of the road."

"What happened?" I blurt out.

He looks surprised by my question. Maybe I shouldn't have asked, but we've been shoveling for over an hour. We've bonded through our manual labor.

"Well," he says, "she got sick." He hesitates a moment. "She has MS. Multiple sclerosis. She has this progressive subtype, and it's just been downhill the last five years. She can't even walk anymore, and I've been mostly taking care of her."

"Oh no," I murmur. "That's terrible. I'm so sorry." But there's a part of me that's relieved he didn't confess his wife has paranoid schizophrenia. Instead, she is too impaired to even leave her house. It doesn't sound like there's any reason to be afraid of her, even if she's the jealous type.

"I wanted her to keep running the restaurant," he says. "I said we could pay to modify the kitchen so she could use it in a wheelchair. But she never wanted to. She's just stuck on wanting to do things the way she's always done them, and if she can't…"

"People can be stubborn."

He nods. "I get that it's hard for her. I'm not saying I would've taken it well if the same thing happened to me. But she could still do everything she used to do if she wanted to. Instead, she doesn't want to do *anything* anymore. She just stays in the house all day, even though she's going crazy in there. It's driving *me* crazy."

I flash him a sympathetic look, thinking of Derek. "We all go a little crazy sometimes."

"Right, but…" He puts down the shovel for a moment and looks off in the distance, at his small house. "It's a lot. On me. It's hard."

"I get it." I bite my lip. "Have you ever thought maybe she would be better off… at another place somewhere?"

There's a sudden flash of anger in his mild brown eyes. "Another *place*? You mean like a *nursing home*?"

"Well…"

"She's my fucking *wife*." His gloved hand turns into a fist. "She's only thirty-five. I'm not sticking her in a *nursing home*. Are you kidding me? What kind of person do you think I am?"

I take a step back, my grip tightening around the shovel. "I'm sorry. I didn't mean it like that. I was just…"

I didn't even realize I was holding my breath until Nick's shoulders sag. "No, *I'm* sorry. I shouldn't have jumped on you. You didn't mean any harm. I shouldn't have been complaining. It's my fault."

I'm shocked how quickly the fight went out of him. If this were Derek, it would have been the start of him screaming at me for hours and mentally torturing me for days. When I dared tell him once that his mother's casserole was too salty, he changed the locks on the front door so I couldn't get in the next day. (And believe me, that casserole was essentially a salt lick.)

"It's okay," I say. "You probably don't get to talk to people much out here."

"That's for sure." He smiles crookedly. "Anyway, thanks for listening. We're relatively happy out here. I mean, things could be better. But it could be worse too, right?"

"Sure," I say. *You could be on the run after killing your husband. Or maybe you didn't kill him, and he's coming after you. So yes, things could be worse.*

"Oh hey," he says. "I think that's my phone ringing."

"I don't hear anything."

"It's on silent. I feel it buzzing." He pulls off his right glove, revealing pink fingers. He digs around in his pocket and pulls out his phone. "Hey, Rosie. What's wrong?"

I watch his expression change as his wife speaks to him. He turns and takes a few steps away from the car. His voice is lower this time but I can still barely make it out. "I'm just helping her dig out her car," he murmurs. "She's stuck in the…" He ducks his head down. "No……… Rosie, come on, that's not…" He lets out a long sigh. "What do you want me to do? I have to help."

I wince. Greta was right—it looks like I've gotten him into trouble with his wife.

He lowers his voice a few more notches, and now I'm having trouble hearing him. Finally, he hangs up the phone. For a moment, he looks annoyed, but then he shakes it off.

"Sorry if I got you in trouble," I say.

He waves his hand. "It's fine. Do you want to try the car? See if you can get it going?"

I look doubtfully at my Corolla. We have gotten all the snow off of the car, but we're still basically sitting in an ocean of snow. How am I supposed to drive out of here? But

I'm willing to give it a try. I don't have to get that far.

I slide into the driver seat. I thought it would be a bit warmer inside the car, but somehow it's even colder. I say a Hail Mary, stick the key in the ignition, and I'm relieved when the engine turns over. I was worried the car died overnight.

But then I hit the gas. And the car doesn't budge.

I roll down the window. "It's not moving at all."

Nick nods thoughtfully. "Okay, put it back in park. Let me dig your wheels out a little more. Then we'll try again."

I wait patiently while he digs my wheels out. After a few minutes, he motions to me to try the car again.

This time, the wheels move forward. I cheer internally for about two seconds, then I'm stuck again. My wheels are spinning, but I'm not going anywhere. I push down harder on the gas, but it's not enough.

"Damn it!" I cry.

Nick frowns. "I'm sorry, Kelly. I just don't think it's going to be possible for me to dig you a trail from here back to the main road. It's pretty far."

"I know," I mumble.

"And like I said, the snow plows will be here this afternoon. I'll make sure they plow around the restaurant so you can get out."

There's nothing I can do about it. We are snowed in until the plow comes. And God knows when that will be. He claims it will be in the afternoon, but when? How many hours am I going to sit around, a sitting duck in a motel room?

And that's when the tears jump into my eyes.

"Kelly?" Nick bends down beside the window. "Are you okay?"

I do my best to wipe the tears away. But he knows what's happening. "I'm okay. I just… I have to be somewhere."

"I wish I could take you. But my Ford would do even worse than your car…"

I blink, unable to keep the tears from spilling over. It wouldn't help if Nick drove me somewhere anyway. I can't leave my car behind. I at least need it for a trade-in. "It's fine."

Nick is quiet for a moment, standing outside the car. He rifles around in his pocket, and I think he's going for his phone, but then he pulls out a wad of tissues. He hands them to me. "They're clean. I promise."

I accept the tissues, wiping my eyes off and struggling to get myself back under control. I can't let myself lose it. This isn't that big a deal. If the roads are snowed in, hopefully the police won't be looking for me too hard either. I've got a few hours. Maybe the plow will come early.

I get out of the car and we trudge back to the hotel together. He's still got the bucket set up on the floor in front of the main counter. I guess he never got around to fixing that leak in Room 201.

I notice now that the water dripping from the ceiling doesn't look clear the way water usually does. It has a brownish tinge. Almost reddish. I wonder if that's from rust. It makes sense that the pipes would be rusty here.

"I'm going to wait for a plumber," Nick says when he sees me looking at the dripping water. "I gave it a go this morning and… well, I'm not having much luck. I think I need a professional, you know?"

I nod. I look at the water accumulating in the bucket. It definitely looks red. That's so strange.

"I'm going up to my room," I say. "I'm going to lie down a bit. All that shoveling made me tired."

"Sure." He goes behind the counter and sits down. "I'm going to catch up on some paperwork, but call me if you want me to make you lunch."

I almost make a joke about big portions, but it dies on my tongue. I'm not in the mood for making jokes right now. I'm also not in the mood for eating.

"I'll let the boots dry out on the radiator, then I'll bring them down to you later," I tell him.

He shrugs. "You may as well keep them. Like I said, Rosalie can't walk anymore anyway. She doesn't need them."

I raise an eyebrow. "So she's okay with you just giving them to me?"

He opens his mouth, but he doesn't say anything right away. "Yeah. You're right. You should probably give them back."

I feel guilty about the wet footprints I leave on the stairs as I tromp back up to my room. Maybe it's the weight of the boots, but the stairs are even creakier this time around. I wouldn't be surprised if they just collapsed in one gigantic pile of rubble.

As I walk back to my room, I pass room 201. I don't know what it is, but every time I walk by this room, I get the chills. The door is closed, and there is a "DO NOT DISTURB" sign hanging from the door knob, even though the room is empty. I press my ear against the door. It's silent inside.

I reach out my hand and brush my fingers against the door. On an impulse, I lower my hand onto the door knob.

And I try to turn it.

CHAPTER 11

"He keeps it locked."

I nearly jump ten feet in the air at the sound of Greta's voice. I don't know how long she's been watching me, from that little crack between her door and the door frame. I yank my hand off the doorknob.

"Sorry," I mumble.

She arches one of her white eyebrows at me. "Do not apologize to *me*. Nick and Rosalie Baxter own this motel. I do not care what you do."

I wipe my hand on my jeans. "I was just…"

"Curious?"

"I guess." I don't want to talk about the strange leak coming from the ceiling right below room 201. "Anyway."

Greta blinks at me. "You should join me. I'm about to have lunch."

That's when I notice quite a nice smell emanating from Greta's room. A minute ago, I had no appetite whatsoever. But the smell of something actually appetizing reminds me it's time for lunch. And whatever Greta made is much better than another turkey sandwich. Or some brown eggs.

"Are you sure?" I ask.

"I would not invite you if I did not want you to come." That is true.

I drop off my coat and boots in my room, then I head to room 202 to join Greta for lunch. Of course, the second I walk into her room, I'm reminded of why it gave me the creeps last time I was here. If I had remembered all the mirrors, I might have said no.

She has a small table set up in front of her bed. I sit down on the edge of the bed and watch as she scoops what looks like a dark brown stew onto a nest of egg noodles.

"Is that goulash?" I ask.

"No," she says. "This is porkolt."

"Porkolt?"

She shakes her head vigorously. "No, *porkolt*."

I'm never going to say it right, so I just nod. She is heaping an enormous amount of stew onto my plate— easily enough for three people. She plops it down in front of me, along with a slightly bent fork.

"It's a lot of food," I comment.

"Yes. You are too skinny. Eat it all."

If I tried to eat all this food, I would probably vomit it

up immediately after. But I'm not going to argue. I dip my fork into the food and spear a hunk of meat. I lift it to my mouth and take a tentative bite. "This is good!"

"Why are you so surprised?"

"It's just…" I take another bite. Maybe I could eat the whole plate. "Where did you make this? You couldn't have made it in this room."

"I made it in the kitchen. Nick lets me use it, and he takes me out to the grocery store once a week. I do not care for his cooking and he does not care to cook."

I take another bite. This is fantastic. It's got this rich stew flavor, and then a hint of paprika. If I made this at home, Derek would…

Oh God, what am I thinking? I'm not making any meals for Derek again. Ever.

"So what was it like working at a carnival?" I ask.

"It was a living." She shrugs as she settles down next to me with her own heaping plate of stew. I don't know how she eats so much when she's so tiny. "I have a gift, so it was my obligation to share it."

"What is your gift… exactly?"

She smiles thinly. "You are skeptical."

I shrug.

"It runs in my family." She stirs the food on her plate. "We all have an ability to see beyond what is visible to the naked eye. I can see past, present, and future."

I chew on a hunk of meat. I have no idea what animal

this is, but it's delicious. "Mmm."

"You should let me tell your fortune."

"I'd rather not."

"Why not? You do not believe in it anyway. So do it for a laugh. Yes?"

I nod at the dresser where I saw the Tarot cards. "So you use Tarot cards or a crystal ball or…?"

She waves a hand dismissively. "Those are just ornaments for putting on a show." She taps her temple. "The real gift is in here."

"Did you tell Nick's fortune?" I ask.

She takes a bite of the stew. "I did."

"And?"

She clucks her tongue. "Whatever happens during a session is private. But I will tell you this. He did not believe his fortune. And that was to his detriment. Also, I will tell you…" She leans in close enough that I can smell wine on her breath. "If Christina Marsh had listened to her fortune, she would still be breathing today."

A hunk of meat feels like it has gotten lodged in my throat. "I think I'll pass on the fortune-telling."

She shrugs. "That is your choice. But even if you do not know your fortune, that does not keep it from coming true."

"If you know your fortune, are you able to stop it? Or do you just have to try to look surprised when it happens?"

"In some cases, people may alter their destinies," she

says. "But it is rare. Most people simply allow it to happen. Like Christina."

I want to roll my eyes at her, because it's also ridiculous. But there's something about this woman. Something about her strange room and her eye socks and her beef stew that is the best thing I've ever tasted in my life. If anyone can tell the future, it's this woman.

And that's all the more reason for me to refuse.

CHAPTER 12

I spend nearly two hours in Greta's room. She tells me more about her time in the carnival—she's actually quite entertaining. She has me laughing out loud at the story about how the carnies fought the mandatory daily shower rule by having a shower strike that lasted a grueling two months.

"By the end," Greta says, "I had to walk around with a clothespin on my nose. Have you ever tried to read somebody's palm with a clothespin on your nose?"

"I can't say I have," I say.

"I do not recommend it."

"Did you have your own room there?"

She adjusts her billowy white nightgown. "I shared a room with Bernie. He was my husband."

"Oh." I swallow. "I didn't realize you were…"

She continues to play with the fabric of her nightgown. "We met at the carnival. I was only nineteen when I met him. I didn't speak much English. He taught me. We were together for over thirty years."

"Was he psychic too?"

She smiles distantly. "Oh no. He did not have the gift. He would run games or rides for them or whatever they needed. We were not blessed with any of our own, but he loved the children who came to the carnival. He loved seeing the smiles on their faces. And then…"

I bite the inside of my cheek. "What?"

"One morning, he did not wake up. The doctors said it was his heart." One side of her lips quirks up although her eyes are wet. "Bernie liked his corn dogs and curly fries. You did not have to be a psychic to know it would do him in. But I am grateful for the years we had together."

I feel an irrational stab of envy. I can see on Greta's face how much she loved this man. I never felt that way about Derek. I'm not sure if I'll ever feel that way about a man. Somehow, true love has eluded me. Maybe I'm immune to it.

"Do not worry." Greta's voice breaks into my thoughts. "You will find love. I promise you."

I cock my head to the side. "Is that what you see in my future?"

"No. You are young and beautiful. Some things are simply obvious."

Right, but she does not know my past. She does not know what I'm running away from. If she knew, she might not be so optimistic about my future.

The thought of what I left behind makes Greta's delicious lunch churn in my stomach. I should not be sitting here chit chatting with an old woman. I've got to get back on the road. I look down at my watch. "I should check in with Nick. Maybe the plow has arrived."

"No. It has not."

"But maybe—"

"I am able to hear the plow through my window. Trust me—it has not arrived."

I wipe my hands on my jeans and get to my feet. "I better get going anyway. But... thank you for lunch. Would you like me to bring the plates downstairs to the kitchen?"

"No, please don't bother yourself. Nick will fetch them later." She arches an eyebrow. "Are you sure you will not let me read your fortune?"

I hesitate. It was a firm no before, but I've gotten to know Greta. I like her. And she seems to really want to do this. So why not? It's better than sitting around my room, pacing back-and-forth as I wait for the plow to arrive.

"Okay," I say. "Sure. Go for it."

Greta smiles at me. "You will not regret this."

That remains to be seen.

She reaches out to dim the yellow lamp by her bed. And now the room is strictly mood lighting. I am sitting beside her on the bed, and she reaches out to take my hands in hers. Her skin feels so delicate, like tissue paper.

"Relax your mind," she instructs me.

"How do I relax my mind?"

"Clear out all thoughts. Make your mind blank."

Easier said than done. "Okay…"

She closes her eyes, but I keep mine open. She tilts her head back and her eyelids flutter. "Yes. You are very accessible to read. You are an open book."

Oh. Wonderful.

"I see…" Her eyelids flutter again. "There is a man in your past. A very handsome man."

"Yes…" I'm not impressed quite yet. There are plenty of handsome men out there.

"Yes, yes…" Her fingers apply pressure to mine. "He was somebody you loved, but you don't love him anymore. He is…"

My breath catches in my throat, and I'm suddenly hanging on her every word.

"You are frightened of this man." Her eyes crack open. "You feel he means to bring you harm."

I swallow. "Well…"

"But the question is," she goes on, "will he? What lies in the future for you and the handsome man?"

The pressure of her fingers on mine grows uncomfortable. I want to pull my hands away but I don't dare break the spell. Suddenly, she lets go of my hands and jumps away from me, like I'm made of fire. Her eyes fly open. "You must go!"

"What?" I stare at her uneasily. "What are you talking about?"

She takes a step back, like she's almost afraid of me. "You go now. You… you are… danger."

I stand up, my legs trembling beneath me. "You mean I'm *in* danger?"

"I'm sorry." She backs up again until she hits the wall. Or the mirror, as it were. "You must go now, Quinn. Go! Go out of here!"

"But…"

"Get out!" she shrieks. "You must go! Get away from this place!"

The veins are standing out in her neck, and her eyes are bulging out in their sockets. I don't even understand what's happening. Why is she freaking out like this? It was *her* idea to tell my fortune!

I'm afraid she's going to start throwing things at me, so I obediently stumble out of her room.

For a moment, I linger in the hallway, stunned. Was that for real? Or was it all a performance, like Nick said? I can't even tell.

Then something hits me.

She called me Quinn. Somehow, she knew my name.

All right, now I'm officially freaked out. I definitely never told her my name. I said I was Kelly, and she called me on it being a fake name, but I never corrected her. So how did she know my name is Quinn?

I close my eyes and I can still see her panicked face. The veins standing out in her neck and on her temples. Screaming at me: *Go! Get out of here!*

What does she think is going to happen if I stay here? What horrible thing did she see in my future?

This is ridiculous. She has to tell me the truth. This isn't fair.

I knock on her door. Then I knock a second time. Then a third.

Okay, she's obviously not answering.

I have a sick, horrible feeling in my stomach. I don't know what she saw in my future or if any of this is real, but I agree with her on one thing: I need to get out of this place. *Now.* I'll go sit in my car until the plow gets here if I have to.

I return to my room and throw everything back into my luggage. It doesn't take very long. Regretfully, I leave the boots behind in the room. I'll have to do what I can with my sneakers.

As I take one last look at the room, I look out the window at the house across the way. The sun is still up, so it's hard to see, but I can just barely make out the shadow of a woman sitting in the window on the second floor.

Rosalie.

I wonder why she's on the second floor. If she can't

walk, why wouldn't she want to stay on the first floor? Why would she trap herself upstairs?

I shake my head. There's no point in thinking about this anymore. Nick's wife isn't my problem anymore. And I'm sure she'll be happy I'm gone.

I take the stairs down as quickly as I can go. It's hard with my bulky luggage, but I need to get out of here. I've got this horrible feeling I don't have much time.

Nick is at the front desk when I come down. He sucks in a breath when he sees me with my luggage. "What are you doing, Kelly?"

"I… I have to go."

He frowns. "But the plow isn't here yet. I told you I would call you when they came."

"I can't wait anymore." I heave my bag onto my shoulder. "I have to get out of here. I'll wait in the car until they arrive."

"But it's freezing out there. What are you going to do? Run the heat for the next two hours? Your car is going to die."

He has a reasonable point. But I can't stay here. "Maybe they'll be here sooner."

"No, they won't. They called me and told me they're delayed. They might not be here for *hours*."

I'm struggling not to burst into tears. "Well, I can't stay here."

"Why not?"

"Because…" I let my heavy bag drop onto the floor. "Greta told me that… She read my fortune and said that I'm in danger."

Nick just stares at me for a moment. Then he bursts out laughing. "Are you serious? I'm sorry, but… really? That's not really why you're leaving, is it?"

"It was…" I dig my thumbnail into my palm. "It was creepy. She seemed to know things about me. And even she seemed freaked out. It felt… real."

"Well, it wasn't. Believe me."

"But—"

"It. Wasn't. Real." He says it with such conviction, it's hard not to believe him. "She's a performer. That's what she used to do for many years. She's not psychic. Come on, Kelly. That's crazy."

"It felt real," I insist.

He shrugs. "That's because she's good at it. You know what she does? It's called cold reading. She told me about it once. She watches you as she says things and looks for subtle cues in your facial expression and body language that tell her she's on the right track. She did it for a living for thirty years. She's *really* good at it."

"I… I don't know."

"Yeah, but *I* know, and I'm telling you. That's what she does."

I look down at my luggage next to my sneakers. I want to believe that was all a performance. I don't want to go sit in my cold car, waiting for that plow to come.

"It's very easy," Nick insists. "Even *I* could do it. Watch." He shuts his brown eyes and massages his temples with his fingertips. "I'm looking into your past. I'm seeing… a man. A very attractive man. Your husband."

I stare at him. "That's exactly what she said."

The left side of his lips quirks up. "Right. Well, you came in here wearing a wedding ring. And obviously, you think your own husband is attractive. So…"

"Yes, but…"

He massages his temples again. "And now I'm seeing a horrible fight between you. Something terrible. And now… now you're running away…"

I take a step back. "How did you…?"

He shrugs. "You're not wearing your ring anymore. And come on, you're *obviously* running away from something. I've never seen anyone so panicked." He looks me in the eyes. "You're pretty easy to read… *Kelly*. I don't need to be psychic."

I take a deep breath, steadying myself by clutching the desk. Maybe he's right. Maybe I'm overreacting to something that was obviously a performance. Maybe I told Greta my name without realizing it. It's certainly something I could've done unconsciously.

"Okay," I say. "I… I guess I'll wait for the plow."

He nods. "That's a good idea. I *promise* I'll call you as soon as they get here."

"Okay, thanks." I take another deep breath. "I appreciate your kindness."

"You're going to be okay." He reaches out and puts his hand on mine. His fingers are a little rough and calloused, unlike Derek's baby smooth skin. For a moment, a thrill goes through me. But then he pulls his hand away. "Just hang out upstairs. You'll be out of here before you know it."

I take my bag and trudge back up the stairs. Despite his reassurances, something is telling me I'm making a horrible mistake by staying here.

CHAPTER 13

When I get back up to my room, there isn't much to do. Since I slept so horribly, I lie down on the bed and shut my eyes. Maybe I could get a bit of sleep in, so that I can drive all night long. After staying in one place for so long, I need to put some distance between me and my home. Fast.

I drift in and out of sleep for a couple of hours. Every time I get into any sort of deep sleep, the image of Derek with the red stain spreading across his abdomen pops into my head. And then I'm wide awake.

That will haunt me for the rest of my life.

I wish I had my phone. If not to make a call, then at least to surf the web. You don't realize how much you depend on your phone for entertainment until it's gone. I wish I had at least brought a book.

I open the top drawer of the dresser. The Bible is apparently the only book in this room. And it's not exactly easy reading. When I was younger, our parents used to make us go to church every Sunday. Claudia and I hated it. We would spend the entire time whispering to each other until our parents told us to be quiet.

Maybe it will give me some comfort. Who knows?

I crack open the Bible. I expect to see the familiar first words: *In the beginning God created the heavens and the earth.*

Instead, the entire first page is covered in red magic marker. Somebody has scribbled across the pages: *Get out now, whore!*

I stare at the words, a prickling sensation in the back of my spine. I turn the page and there it is again. The same words, written over and over. *Get out get out get out get out…*

I snap the Bible shut with shaking hands. Well, so much for getting comfort from the words of God.

I wonder if those words were meant for me. I wonder if somebody saw me by my car with Nick and wanted to send me a message. I raise my eyes and look across at the house next door. The sun has gone down and I can see that same light on the top window. And the silhouette of a woman staring out at me.

Rosalie.

But it couldn't have been her. Nick told me she can't even *walk*. She couldn't have come over here, climbed up the stairs, unlocked the door to my room, scribbled in the Bible, then gone back home. It's impossible.

Anyway, I need to calm down. The plow should be here soon, and then I'll get out of here. And never come back. In the meantime, I'll watch some TV. That should help.

I turn on the television. Unlike yesterday, the picture is clear. There is another pretty blond newscaster on the screen, talking about damage caused by the storm. Stupid storm. If that hadn't happened, I would've been out of here ages ago. But I am praying I still have more time. After all, it's only Saturday. It's entirely possible nobody will notice Derek is missing until Monday.

"In other news," the anchorwoman says, "the body of thirty-four-year-old Derek Alexander was found last night in his home…"

My chest turns to ice. *What?*

The blond anchorwoman keeps talking, but I can only focus on little pieces of what she's saying. And then a second later, Deputy Scott Dwyer is on the screen. He doesn't look great—he looks like he hasn't gotten much more sleep than I have. Scott's mildly bloodshot brown eyes make contact with the camera lens as he recites the details of the case in a flat voice.

Death is from apparent stab wounds… No forced entry… attempting to locate wife Quinn Alexander for questioning…

They found him. They found Derek dead, and now they're looking for me. And according to the newscast, he was found last night. Probably the only reason the police aren't here already is because of the storm. Or maybe I got lucky, and they didn't see the sign for the Baxter Motel.

Which means I don't have much time.

Screw the snow plow. I'm getting out of here. I'll go wait in my car, so I can take off as soon as it's clear to go. At the very least, I can't be hanging around this motel any longer.

I grab my luggage, which is thankfully already packed. I shove my feet back in my sneakers, then I head out of the room, locking the door behind me. I walk over to the staircase, but before I can start descending, I hear voices coming from downstairs.

Oh my God.

It's the police.

CHAPTER 14

I freeze.

I'm not sure what else to do. I want to go back to my room and lock and deadbolt the door, but I'm afraid to move. I knew the police were going to come looking for me, but I didn't think it would happen this quickly. Or at least, I was *hoping* it wouldn't happen this quickly.

"This is your motel, Mr. Baxter?" a deep male voice is asking. I don't recognize the voice, but it's not Scott. If it were Scott, I might come out. Of course, he would arrest me anyway, but he'd be kind about it. He wouldn't make the handcuffs too tight.

"Right, it's my motel." Nick's voice. "I own it. Me and my wife."

"Does anyone else work here?"

"No. It's just me."

"I see. Mr. Baxter, we're looking for a woman named Quinn Alexander, who we think may have stopped at your establishment in the last twenty-four hours. Does this photo look familiar to you?"

I hold my breath. There's a long silence coming from downstairs. Oh God. What am I going to do? Can I jump out the window? How badly would I be hurt?

This is my own fault. I should have left while I had a chance. But where can I go? The plows still haven't come. I would be just as much of a sitting duck in my car as I am here. Although it's possible they might not see the car behind the diner.

It's all over. The police are going to take me away. I'm going to spend the rest of my life in prison.

"Uh, no," Nick is saying. "Doesn't look familiar to me, sorry."

My breath catches in my throat.

The officer's voice again: "Are you sure? She may have changed her hair. It might be shorter than in the photo."

"Yeah, no, I haven't seen her. Honestly, we haven't had any new guests here in the last several days at all."

My shoulders sag. I can't believe it—Nick is covering for me. He's lying to the police on my behalf. He's risking everything to help me, even though he doesn't even know who I am.

"Okay then," the officer says. "You mentioned your wife also works here. Could we talk to her as well? Maybe she saw Mrs. Alexander."

"Unfortunately," Nick says, "my wife has been very

sick recently. She's been in bed the last week. I think it's the flu. You probably don't want to go near her."

The officer chuckles. "I don't suppose I do. All right then. You'll let us know if she shows up?"

"Oh, absolutely."

"Thank you, Mr. Baxter. Appreciate it."

"Sorry I couldn't be more helpful." He pauses. "I hope you find her."

"Oh, we will. It's just a matter of time."

I lean against the wall, my heart pounding. I can't believe that just happened. The police showed up here, just as I feared they would, but somehow I'm not being carried off in handcuffs. Nick covered for me. But that doesn't mean I'm home free.

I wait until I hear the door to the motel slam shut, then I run back to my room. I look out the window—it's very dark out now, but I can make out the police officer getting into his vehicle. I watch as he starts up his car and drives off. And there's one other thing I see.

The plow is here. It's plowing away a path to freedom. That must be how the police car got here. In about fifteen minutes, I may be able to finally leave.

And then I hear a knock at the door.

"It's Nick."

I walk over to the door and crack it open. Nick is standing there, wringing his hands together. I have the irrepressible urge to reach out and hug him.

"Can I come in?" he asks.

I step aside and he enters my room, closing the door behind him. The fleeting thought occurs to me that maybe this wasn't entirely altruistic on his part. Maybe he's here to ask me for money. *Give me five hundred bucks or else I'm going to the police.* Except I don't really think that. He doesn't seem like the type. After all, he didn't even ask for money for the meals he made me.

"You heard that, right?" he says. "The police? Looking for you."

I nod slowly. "Yes, I… thank you. I don't know how I can ever repay you."

He smiles crookedly. "I bet the guy had it coming."

I drop my eyes. "He did. I promise you, he did."

"Yeah, I, uh… I saw those bruises on your neck. Anyway, I just…"

"I'll be okay. Really."

"Okay then." He glances out the window. "The plow arrived just before the police came. So in another fifteen minutes or so, you should be good to go."

I nod again. I don't think I can talk, because I'm going to start crying.

Nick wrings his hands together. "I don't know where you're going. It's better if I don't know. But… is there anything you need? Anything I can do to help?"

Don't cry. Don't cry. "No… thank you."

He looks over at the fur-lined boots I wore earlier

today. It almost feels like a million years ago. "You should keep the boots. Really."

Well, that did it. Now I'm sobbing. I sink down onto the bed, my shoulders shaking as the tears pour down my cheeks. Nick looks a little panicked, but he sits down next to me and rubs my back.

"Hey," he says, "it's okay. I promise. It's going to be okay. I won't tell anyone. Greta won't either."

"I know." I wipe my eyes with the back of my hand. "I just… It's hard to leave everything behind. And you're so… kind to me."

"I'm just trying to help," he says softly.

"I know, but…" I take a shaky breath. "When you've lived with somebody for so long who spends every waking moment plotting how to be cruel to you…"

He frowns. "I'm so sorry, Quinn."

He's calling me by my real name now, which he knows because of the police. The unfairness of it all hits me. Why couldn't I have married a good guy like Nick? Why did I have to vow to spend my life with a narcissistic sociopath?

I look up into his brown eyes with my red, swollen ones. The kindness and concern in his eyes almost floors me. And before I entirely know what I'm doing, I lean forward and I press my lips against his.

CHAPTER 15

The kiss is over almost before it's begun. A split second after my lips make contact with his, Nick jumps away from me like I've just scalded him. He's staring at me, his eyes wide.

"Jesus Christ, Quinn! What are you *doing*?"

I should never have done that. What a horrible mistake. All the kindness and concern has disappeared from his face. "I'm so sorry. I just—"

"I'm *married*." As he says the words, he glances out the window, at his own house across the way. At that one glowing light. "I love my wife, okay? Jesus Christ, what were you *thinking*?"

"I'm sorry. I didn't mean to—"

"You've got to leave." He rakes a hand through his hair. "You've got to get out of here. *Now*."

"Listen, the boots—"

"Take the boots," he says through his teeth. "I don't care about the fucking boots, okay? You've got to go though. I… I covered for you with the police. Now you have to go." He backs up against the door. "Please."

"Yes, of course," I say stiffly. "I'll go now. As soon as the plow is done. Okay? I don't want to make trouble for you."

"Right." His hand grips the doorknob behind him. "Then don't."

With those words, he yanks the door open and gets the hell out of my room.

I didn't think it was possible, but I feel even worse than I did five minutes ago. What was I thinking? The poor guy was just trying to help me, and then I launched myself at him. As he pointed out to me, he's married. All those years, I blamed Derek for cheating on me, and look what I did when I had the chance. I kissed another woman's husband.

And not just another woman. A woman who is ill. Who is counting on him to take care of her, who can't fight back. I am a horrible person. I deserve everything coming to me.

I look back up through the window. That light is still on in the other house. Rosalie Baxter is sitting where she always does. Watching. She must've seen everything. No wonder Nick was so freaked out.

I want to tell her I'm sorry. That it was entirely my fault, not her husband's. He was only trying to be a good guy. I just don't have much experience with good guys lately.

But there's no way for me to apologize. I'm not about to go over there and have a heart-to-heart with the woman. The best thing is to do what Nick said: get out.

I look down at the snow between the motel and the house. I see Nick in his black coat walking across the cleared path. He's going over to talk to her. Probably to apologize.

God, I feel terrible.

All I can do now is sit there and wait for the stupid plow to be done. I can hear it making noises as it scoops the snow away. If only it hadn't snowed like this. I would be hundreds of miles away by now in a remote location in Canada. Instead, I'm trapped here. The police will be on the lookout for my license plate. By now, I should have swapped it out already.

I choke back another sob. There's no way I'm getting out of here. I'm too close to home and the police are going to find me. If not in the next few hours, then in the next few days. I don't know how to get a phony ID, and I don't know how I'm going to make more money if I don't have an ID. This is all going to explode in my face very quickly.

Running away was the wrong thing to do. I wasn't prepared, and I'm not built for it. My best chance is to go back. 'Fess up to what I did.

Nick noticed the bruises on my neck. When the police see them, maybe they'll believe my story. And if I go back, Claudia will be there to support me.

I've made up my mind. I'm going back home.

I won't tell the police where I spent the night. It will get Nick in trouble. I'll say I slept in my car. They won't care. As long as they find me.

I thought I would feel sick at the idea of facing the police and maybe going to jail, but strangely enough, it feels like a great weight off my shoulders. I don't want to run away. I want to tell everybody what I did and why I did it. Derek deserved it. He was a horrible person. A monster. If I hadn't killed him, he would have killed me.

I look out the window—the area around the motel appears to be cleared away. I can leave now—finally. I grab my bag and exit my room one last time. As I lock the door behind me, I see that room 202 has cracked open again. Greta is watching me leave. But as soon as I turn to look at her, she shuts the door tight.

"Bye, Greta," I say.

The stairs creak threateningly as I make my way down to the first floor. My bag strap bites into my shoulder. I consider leaving it in the lobby while I bring the car around, but Nick isn't down here and I don't want to leave it unattended.

The ceiling is still leaking, the same way it was when I came in. Why does the water look so red? I still don't get it. But it's none of my concern. I drop my keys on the desk.

I push the door open to escape the motel. The cold air hits me in the face, but at least it's not snowing. I forgot to zip up my coat, and the wind slips between the folds of my open jacket. At least the roads should be clear by now, especially once I get on the highway. I should be home in two hours. And then I'll turn myself in.

As I rifle through my purse, looking for my keys, I hear footsteps. I look up and see a figure approaching me. It's so dark here, it's hard to see who it is. I squint out into the blackness.

"Hello?" I say.

A raspy voice spits out, "How could you do that?"

And then a second later the knife buries itself in my abdomen, between the open folds of my coat. I stare at it for a moment, watching the crimson stain spread across my shirt. And then everything goes black.

CHAPTER 16

CLAUDIA

One Day Earlier

Every time I ask Deputy Scott Dwyer a question he has one of three answers:

I don't know.

I can't say.

Why don't you go home and I'll call you when we know something?

I find the third one especially maddening. If your baby sister were missing after her husband was found in a pool of blood in their kitchen, would you just go home and *chill* until the incompetent deputy got his head out of his ass?

No, I didn't think so. Unfortunately, the police chief is out of town on vacation and won't be back until Monday. God knows how badly Scotty will muck everything up by then.

"Mrs. Delaney," Scotty says to me as we stand in the freezing rain outside my sister's house. His freckles have faded from when he was in high school and he's bulked up enough to fill out his blue uniform—he used to be passably cute when Quinn was dating him, but now he's grown into someone the housewives love to ogle. "You should go home. We're handling this."

"*Handling* this?" I stare at him. "The same way you *handled* it when you came here a few hours ago, after getting a call from a neighbor that they heard screaming. And instead of looking inside the house, you just *walked away*? Handle it kind of like *that*?"

Scotty's cheeks are pink. It could be because of the cold, but it could also be because he knows he royally screwed up. He was *here*. He was at this house, when my sister was still here and possibly in terrible danger. And he didn't even check it out.

I was the one who discovered the body in the kitchen. It was much later. Too late.

I *knew* something was wrong when I spoke to her on the phone.

"She looked fine when I came to the door," he says. "She said the neighbor just heard a movie."

I don't even know what to say to that. My sister opened

the door for the police officer, and God knows if there was somebody pointing a gun at her head while she gave all the right answers. If Scott had only stepped inside…

"You're sure you don't know who those messages were from?" Scott asks.

"If I did, don't you think I would tell you?" I snap at him.

That's yet another piece in the puzzle. Besides Derek's iPhone, he also had a burner phone in his pocket. Scott claimed that just prior to his death, he was texting with another woman. Planning to meet her for a rendezvous at his house while he believed Quinn to be at work.

"She could be a witness," Scott points out.

"Or she could have killed my sister." I glare at him. "You're examining that possibility, aren't you?"

"Of course," he says. "We're examining every possibility."

There is one thing on Quinn's side here, and that's the fact that I'm pretty sure Scott is still in love with her. It's been a decade since they dated in high school, but he still hasn't gotten married. Doesn't even have a serious girlfriend, from what I've heard. I remember the year after Quinn left for college, Scotty looked like a sad puppy dog every time I saw him. I stopped going into his father's store because every time I did, he would be there sweeping the floor or working the cash register, and he would ask me about Quinn in that hopeful voice.

He was almost obsessed with her.

Another officer is calling to Scott from inside the house. He glances behind him, then back at me. He tries to blink away the frozen raindrops on his pale eyelashes. "I've got to go, Claudia."

"You'll call me if you find out anything?"

"I will. I promise." He pauses. I'm sure it's a lie. "And you'll call me if you hear from Quinn?"

"Of course," I say.

But that's also a lie.

As he walks away, I reach into my purse and pull out my phone for the hundredth time. I select Quinn's number from my favorites list. I let it ring.

And ring.

And ring.

Pick up, dammit. Please, Quinn. It's me. *It's your sister.*

"Hi! You've reached Quinn's phone! Please leave a message at the beep."

I grit my teeth. I didn't expect her to answer, but I'd been hoping. I'm not sure if she even has her phone anymore. If she had it, she would have picked up by now. Even so, I leave another message.

"Quinn, it's Claudia." I grip my phone tighter with my freezing hand. "Please call me back if you get this. *Please.* Whatever happened, we're going to figure it out. I promise you. Just… call me back. I love you."

I hang up the phone. I stare down at the screen, willing

it to ring. But of course, it doesn't.

Right now, Quinn's husband is dead. *Murdered.* Quinn is gone and so is her car.

In my mind, there are two possibilities:

The first is that whoever killed Derek also did something to Quinn. When Scotty showed up at her house, there was somebody hiding behind the door with a gun, ready to shoot her if she said the wrong words. And she's currently tied up in a trunk or in some underground dungeon without access to her phone.

The second possibility is that Quinn is the one who killed Derek.

It's hard to imagine the second possibility. No, Quinn and Derek did not have an ideal marriage. She complained about him a *lot*, to the point where I wasn't sure why she stuck around. But my sister isn't the murdering type. Even when she was a teenager, she couldn't even bear to smash a beetle she found crawling in her bed—she would make me capture it and set it free. Hell, she didn't even like throwing the ball at people during *dodgeball* when we were kids. I can't picture her stabbing her own husband in cold blood and leaving him bleeding to death in the middle of her kitchen. The same kitchen she and I spent hours flipping through magazines together in our attempt to make it into The Perfect Kitchen. She wouldn't. She *couldn't.*

Maybe Quinn wasn't that crazy about Derek, but she had a good life. The idea that she would stab him to death...

I just can't imagine it.

So by process of elimination, that means she's being held captive somewhere. And we've got to find her.

I'm going to find you, Quinn. I triple dipper promise with a cherry on top.

My phone rings and my heart leaps. But then I pull it out of my purse and my face falls when I see the name on the screen. Rob. I jab at the green button to answer the call.

"Claudia." His voice is tight. "Are you coming home?"

I glance over at Scott, who is lingering in the entranceway of the Alexander household. "Not yet."

"The police are handling it. You should come home."

"Everyone here is incompetent."

"Claudia, you're a masseuse! Can you please leave this to the police?"

I may be a masseuse, but I was majoring in criminal justice in college. I might have gone to law school if I had finished. If my parents hadn't lost control of their car that afternoon at the end of my freshman year.

"I want to find my sister," I insist. I'm not going to sit around and let the police screw this up any more than they already have.

At first, I think Rob is going to say something insensitive, but then he redeems himself by instead saying, "Do you want me to meet you over there?"

"No. It's fine."

"It's *not* fine, Claudia. The rain is coming down hard,

and it's turning to snow. All you've got is the Chevy. If you're going to stay, at least let me pick you up in my truck."

Rob and I have been married for almost six years now. Things have gotten kind of stale between us lately, and he's always working—always running out to unclog a toilet somewhere. Sometimes I think Rob and I don't care much for each other anymore. But then he goes and says something like that.

I glance up at my sister's house. The doorstep is slick with ice. Rob is right. It's really coming down.

I see the outline of Scott Dwyer in the window. He's talking to another officer, and it seems to me he is far too calm considering he's investigating a murder. I still can't figure out what he was thinking. He heard screaming coming from my sister's house. Why didn't he go inside and investigate? What kind of police officer doesn't investigate *screaming*? It's strange.

But either way, there's nothing we can do about it now.

"Fine," I say. "I'll come home."

CHAPTER 17

Rob isn't a wealthy entrepreneur like Derek, so our house is much more modest than the one I just came from. Two stories, three bedrooms, two of which aren't much bigger than Quinn's walk-in closet. It was a fixer-upper when we bought it three years ago, and we haven't entirely fixed it up. The outside still needs a good coat of paint. The porch is still unfinished, and six months ago I put my foot right through a floorboard.

Rob is handy, and he always swears he's in the middle of fixing it all. Every Sunday, he gets out his tool belt and acts like he's doing something important, but meanwhile, the front of our house still looks like something out of a gothic horror novel.

I'm dripping wet when I walk into the house through the garage entrance. Standing in the freezing rain for hours will do that to you. But on the drive home, the rain turned into snow—Rob was right. The roads became incredibly slippery, and I had to focus all my attention on getting home safely.

When I get into the living room, I'm pleased to find that Rob has cranked the heat way up. Usually it annoys me when he does that, but now I'm grateful for it.

Rob is sitting on our secondhand sofa, reading the newspaper, although it's probably just the sports page. He might be the only person under the age of fifty who still reads a paper newspaper. And he isn't even forty yet, although he could easily pass for ten years older since he started losing his hair a few years ago.

When he sees me, he tosses the newspaper aside, his fingers coated in a layer of ink. Rob's fingers are always either covered in ink from the paper or covered in grime from his job. I feel like I need to hose him down before he can kiss me hello.

"So what's going on?" he asks. "Do the police have any leads?"

I swallow a lump in my throat. "They're trying to trace her phone. But somehow they can't do it. Something about the weather. They said the storm is messing everything up."

Rob's brow crinkles. "How are *you* doing?"

I take a shaky breath, shivering under my damp clothing. "I can't believe this is all happening. I only just spoke to her this afternoon. I *knew* something was wrong…"

Knew it better than the damn cop.

He comes over to me and massages my shoulder. I let him do it for a second, but then I jerk away when I remember his ink-stained fingers.

"Can you wash your hands please?" I say.

Rob blinks at me. For a moment, I think this is going to be the start of another fight. But then he goes over to the sink and washes his hands. He soaps them up and everything. He's on his best behavior.

"Good thing you went over there to check on her," he says as he rinses off the black tinged soap.

"Yeah," I murmur.

When I close my eyes, I can still see the scene that greeted me when I stepped into the Alexander household hours earlier. I shudder. I'll never forget it for as long as I live.

"Claudia?" I open my eyes. Rob has finished washing his hands and is staring at me. "Are you okay?"

"I…" I shiver, and I'm not sure if it's from the cold. "Maybe I'll go upstairs and take a shower. Is the hot water working?"

He nods. "Should be."

Part of me wishes I had stayed at the crime scene. Maybe I'm just a masseuse, but nobody knows my sister like I do. If anyone could find her, it's me.

But Scotty promised to call me if they find any new

information. I'm terrified the new information will be finding Quinn in a ditch somewhere. I don't know how I'm going to sleep tonight.

I climb the stairs to the master bedroom—the only one of our three bedrooms that isn't pint-sized. When we bought the house, we imagined the other two bedrooms would be for our kids, but no kids have come along yet. So right now, we've got two guestrooms. Not that we get many guests. I told Quinn if she ever left Derek, she could have her pick.

The bed is still made from this morning with the green floral printed bedspread. I make the bed every day after I wake up in the morning. Even though nobody sees our bedroom besides me and Rob, my mother always made us make our beds, and I can't leave the bedroom with the bed still unmade. I just *can't*. And I would die of shock if Rob ever made the bed.

While I'm stripping off my wet clothing, my phone rings. Again, my heart leaps, hoping it's some sort of news about the case or maybe Quinn herself calling. But instead, the name on the screen is Lori Marshall.

I only have Lori's phone number programmed into my phone because I gave her a massage a few times. But I stopped taking her calls after Quinn told me she was pretty sure Lori was having an affair with Derek. She's exactly his type. Blond with legs longer than the Empire State Building. He loves blondes. That's why Quinn started coloring her hair.

Why would Lori be calling now?

I consider letting it go to voicemail, but curiosity gets the better of me. So I answer the phone. "Lori?"

"Hi, Claudia." I can tell from the hushed tone of her voice that she knows what happened. I didn't see any reporters around, so I assume it isn't on the news yet, but it must have spread through word-of-mouth. "I... I heard the news. Is it true?"

"Is what true?" I ask drily.

"You know, about..." Her voice breaks. "Derek. That he's been... *killed.*"

I consider denying the whole thing, but she'll know the truth soon enough. "Yes. It's true."

Lori lets out a strangled sob. "Oh, how awful! How could Quinn do something like that?"

"Excuse me," I hiss into the phone. "But my sister is *missing*, and I don't appreciate your assumptions."

"Your sister killed her husband then ran away! What other conclusion can you draw?"

"You know..." I lower myself onto my bed. "The police have a reason to suspect Derek was meeting another woman this afternoon."

"He... he was?"

"That's right." I clear my throat. "Tell me, Lori, are you still sleeping with Derek?"

"Claudia! What are you saying?"

"I think you know what I'm saying."

"Well, that's just preposterous!" She's trying to sound indignant, but I can hear the tremor in her voice. "I think the police should focus their energy on locating Quinn."

"Actually," I say, "I don't care what you think, Lori. Expect to be hearing from the police."

I hang up the phone and drop it down onto the center of the bed. Back when I was a kid, we used to have a real phone. A landline. And when you were mad at someone, you could slam it down. It's just not the same with a cell phone.

As much as I dislike that woman, I don't genuinely think she knows what happened to my sister. She's just a busybody. She's the sort of person who would take pleasure seeing Quinn on trial for what happened to Derek. And she wouldn't be the only one. Derek was eminently likable. As well as rich and powerful.

The phone rings again. If it's another one of Derek's mistresses, I swear I'm going to lose it. But when I look over at the screen, I see a name I didn't expect.

It's Quinn.

CHAPTER 18

I scoop up the phone, my hands shaking so badly I can barely swipe to answer. *Don't hang up, Quinn! I just need to get my fingers working again.*

Finally, the call connects. I gasp into the phone, "Quinn?"

I expect to hear my sister's high, sweet voice. Instead, I hear a much deeper voice. "Hello?"

My breath catches in my throat. It's a man. A man is calling on Quinn's phone. Does that mean he's kidnapped her? And he's going to demand ransom?

"Who is this?" I manage.

There's a long pause on the other line. "Who is *this*?"

What is going on here? "Why are you on my sister's phone?"

"I found this phone," the male voice tells me. "It was

in the back of my truck."

I frown, not sure what to make of this development. "The back of your truck? What are you talking about?"

"I was getting something out of my truck and I saw the phone in there. And there were all these missed calls from somebody named Claudia. Is that you?"

"That's me."

"I don't know how the phone got in my truck, but I'd be happy to return it."

He poses an excellent question. How did the phone get in his truck?

I spoke with Quinn on the phone, so it was in her possession when we were talking. Shortly after that, I discovered Derek's dead body. At that point, she was no longer answering her phone. So sometime between our call and when I found Derek, the phone ended up in this guy's car.

The real question is, is this guy on the level? Or is he just messing with me? If I go retrieve the phone from him, will he hit me on the head and try to stuff me in his closet?

I'd like to see him try. Unlike Quinn, I'm a fighter.

"Who is your sister?" the guy asks.

"Her name is Quinn. She—"

"Wait—Quinn Mackey?"

There's a note of surprise and eagerness in his voice. Also, he used our maiden name. I realize at this moment that this man did not do anything terrible to my sister. He's just a guy who found her phone in his truck.

"That's right," I say. "Do you know her?"

"Yeah! My name is Bill Walsh. She used to babysit for me years ago, and I actually saw her earlier today. At a gas station maybe half an hour north of here."

I suck in a breath. "You saw her? When?"

"Um. I'm not sure. Maybe five o'clock? I had just finished work."

My heart is pounding. He saw Quinn. He saw her after our phone call. "Was she alone?"

"Seemed to be. She bought a few things at the store, I think she took out some money, then she ran off. She seemed to be in a big hurry."

"There was nobody else in the car?"

"Not that I could see."

I chew on my lower lip. "How did she look? Did she look… nervous? Scared? Hurt?"

He thinks about it for a moment. "Now that you mention it, she seemed kind of nervous. But she looked good otherwise. *Really* good."

Great. This idiot was hitting on my sister. "Is the phone locked?"

"Yeah. I could only call you because your phone call was on the lock screen."

That means even if I get my hands on the phone, I won't be able to do much with it. "Look," I say, "I'm going to call the police about the phone. They're going to come pick it up from you."

"The police?" Bill Walsh sounds panicked. "But I didn't steal it! I found it in my truck. I swear…"

"I know. But… Quinn is missing."

His breath hitches. "You don't think that I…"

I don't. My gut is telling me this guy is just an innocent passerby. Quinn wanted to get rid of her phone so she couldn't be tracked, so she tossed it in his truck. It's what I would've done. I'm proud of her for thinking on her feet.

And that means Quinn isn't being held captive somewhere. She left on her own volition. Probably right after she stabbed Derek to death.

This changes everything.

It means that if the police find Quinn, she's going straight to jail. It means this is a manhunt, not a rescue mission.

The right thing to do—the *legal* thing to do—would be to call Scott Dwyer and tell him this new piece of information. He's in charge of this investigation, and this is a significant piece of evidence.

But I don't trust Scott. I don't know what he's going to do when he finds out that Quinn was alive and well and *alone* right after her husband was stabbed. But it won't be good for Quinn.

I can't let that happen. I have to play this right.

"Well, you could see how this looks," I say. "A woman goes missing and you mysteriously have her phone. Doesn't look good for you, Bill."

"But I just found it in my truck," he says in a tiny voice. "I swear, I didn't touch her."

"I hope for your sake the police believe that story."

"Shit," I hear him mutter under his breath. "I… I don't know what to say. I'm a good guy. I'd never hurt a woman. And… Christ, my girlfriend would kill me if she thought I…"

"Look," I say. "I believe you. I'm just not sure the police will."

"Well, maybe I could give you back the phone and you don't have to tell them…"

I glance at the door to the bedroom. Rob is still downstairs—I'd rather he not hear this. "Tell you what, Bill. Why don't I come by and get the phone from you. I'll bring it to the police tomorrow and I won't tell them you were involved."

"You would do that?"

"Sure. I can tell from your voice you're an honest man. I just want to find out what happened to my sister."

"Me too," he says earnestly. "Quinn was a nice girl. She was my favorite babysitter. I… I hope you find her."

"Me too." I'm *going to* find her. And I'm going to find her before the police do.

"So can you come by tonight?"

I glance out the window. The snow is really coming down. If I leave now, Rob will have a fit. He'll want to know where I'm going, and I'll have to have a damn good answer. "I'll come first thing in the morning. In the meantime, just power the phone down. If it's off, nobody can track it."

"Got it."

I wonder how old Bill Walsh is. He's younger than Quinn, if she babysat for him. Maybe early twenties. He sounds like a kid who will do anything I say. If I say it the right way.

"I'll come by tomorrow morning," I promise. "Just give me your address."

CHAPTER 19

I don't sleep very well.

I drift in and out of slumber, dreaming of Quinn. I remember the first time I saw her. Our parents told me I was going to get a new baby sister, and then one day they brought me to the hospital, and there she was. This tiny little scrunched up newborn lying in my mother's arms. I wanted so badly to hold her, but they wouldn't let me. They said I was too little.

Except when both of them were gone, I was the one who took care of Quinn. When I got the call about the accident, I dropped everything. I had exams the next day, but nothing else seemed important anymore. I left school and got a job so we could keep the house. I was all she had. And she was all I had.

She should've listened to me about Derek Alexander. I told her he wasn't right for her. I've made every mistake in the book, so I should know. Obviously, I didn't know this exact thing was going to happen. I didn't know Derek was going to end up dead in the kitchen of their expensive home. But I knew she shouldn't marry him.

Well, too late for that now.

I wake up at the crack of dawn. It's Saturday, so Rob is sleeping in. He's lying on his side of the bed, his mouth hanging open, a bit of drool sliding out of the left corner of his lips as he snores loudly. My husband snores like a chainsaw. I showed him an article once about that disordered sleep breathing thing, where you stop breathing during your sleep, and people who snore loudly are more likely to have it.

It means every night you stop breathing in your sleep, Rob, I told him.

You really believe that bullshit? he shot back. And he threw the article in the trash.

I get dressed as quietly as I can and go downstairs. When I look out the window, our entire driveway is caked in at least a foot of snow. I put on my heaviest winter boots, and I take the keys to the truck out of the little basket by the door. My Chevy won't make it, but Rob's rusty green truck will do the trick.

Bill Walsh lives only a fifteen minute drive from my house. I found his profile last night on Facebook—he's a big guy in his twenties like I thought, who sports a goofy expression in most of his photos. He looks utterly harmless, and I don't think I'll have much trouble wrangling the phone away from him. I'm sure he'll be happy to hand it over.

The roads in our town are still slippery with snow. I haven't called the police station yet today, but I'm guessing they haven't made much progress on finding Quinn. If they found her, I would know. My guess is she's hunkering down somewhere for the night. The question is, where?

Bill's house is even smaller than mine and even more badly in need of a coat of paint. I park right in front, and as soon as I get out of the car, my boots sink deep into the snow. I take a good minute to get to his front door. It's like walking through molasses.

My coat isn't warm enough for the icy breeze in the air, and I hug my chest as I wait for Bill to answer the door. After only a few moments, the door swings open like he's been waiting for me. The guy towers over me, but there's something young and vulnerable about his face and the scrap of a goatee on his chin.

"Claudia?" he says quietly.

I nod. "You got the phone?"

He hesitates a moment, then he holds it out to me. Quinn's iPhone. Before he can change his mind, I snatch it out of his hand. It's been powered down, just like I told him.

He scratches at his flimsy goatee. "You won't tell the police?"

"I'll keep my mouth shut."

"Thanks." He shifts his weight. "I want to help find her

and all. I really do. But the thing is, I'm on probation right now. So I can't—"

I get an uneasy feeling in my stomach. Maybe I shouldn't have been so quick to protect this guy. "You're on probation?"

"Me and my buddy were selling weed."

I look down at the phone in my hand. If I go to the police, I'll be in more trouble than he'll be in. But he doesn't need to know that. "Don't worry about it. We'll keep it between us."

His shoulders sag. "Thanks. I appreciate it. And I hope you find Quinn. She was awesome."

I lift my eyes to look into his. "You swear she seemed okay to you? Not hurt?"

"Not hurt." He cocks his head to the side. "But she seemed... It was like something wasn't right. She was nervous about something. In a hurry."

"Thanks." I squeeze the phone in my hand. "This will be very helpful. And I won't say a word about you to the police. I don't want you to get thrown in jail again."

I said that last part just to make sure he keeps his damn mouth shut.

I stomp back out to the truck and shut myself inside it, before my fingers go numb. I sit for a moment in the driver seat, staring at the phone that Quinn tried so hard to get rid of.

Now I've got to do it for her.

CHAPTER 20

In our small New England town, one thing that never stops regardless of the weather is funerals.

There's a cemetery about an hour west of home. The opposite direction of where Quinn was headed. It's a cemetery I know very well.

Because it's where our parents are buried.

They died when I was eighteen and Quinn was fourteen. A car accident took them both. They were driving to the high school to see a school play that Quinn was starring in. They spun out of control on the snowy road and collided with a tractor trailer. They were both killed instantly.

Unfortunately, money was tight before the accident, and they let their insurance policy lapse. So Quinn and I were left with nothing. It was a no-brainer to quit college. I couldn't pay for school anymore anyway, and I couldn't let Quinn be sent to live with distant relatives, or worse, end up in foster care with strangers.

From then on, it was just me and Quinn against the world. I looked out for her, made sure she studied for her exams, hung out with the right kids, and vetted her rare boyfriends. Too bad she didn't listen to me about the man she married.

I hardly ever think about our parents anymore. It's been an eternity since they died. I can't even imagine the sound of my mother's voice anymore. I forget whether my father had a beard or not. It feels like I knew them in another lifetime. But I still come here sometimes. I bring flowers.

But that's not why I'm here today.

Sure enough, when I arrive at the cemetery, there's a funeral going on, despite the snow. The funeral procession is parked along the side of the road, and the mourners are gathered around the gravestone. They're bundled up in heavy coats and hats, as they say goodbye to their loved one a final time.

I sit in my car for a moment, then I power up Quinn's phone. I see the little Apple logo appear on the screen, and a second later, the phone prompts me to enter a passcode.

What would Quinn choose as her passcode? Her birthday? I try it, but no luck. My birthday? That doesn't work either.

My own phone buzzes. It's Rob, texting me: *Where did you go with my truck???*

I don't answer. Instead, I type in Derek's birthday.

And now I'm locked out.

It doesn't matter. I didn't come here to get into Quinn's phone. I came here to get rid of it.

My phone buzzes again. I don't even look at it. I'm sure it's Rob.

I walk along the row of parked cars. Most of them are locked up tight, but a couple have their windows cracked open. I come to a stop when I see a car with Vermont license plates. The back window is cracked open just a hair. Just enough for me to slide Quinn's phone in.

There. Let's see Scott track her down now.

I look back up at the cemetery. I haven't been here for at least a year. At first, Quinn and I used to come here every month. I would drive us and we would stand together in front of their headstones, holding hands. Quinn would usually cry. She blamed herself. After all, they had been going to see her play.

If only I hadn't tried out for that stupid play, she would sob.

After a while, we started going every other month. Then every few months. Then once a year.

Well, I guess that means it's time for a visit.

I step through the iron gates to get into the cemetery. The snow is mostly untouched in here. It's thick and flawlessly white. My legs sink almost to my knees as I walk over to our parents' gravestones.

They're all the way in the back. Maxine Turner Mackey and Samuel Mackey. Beloved wife and husband, parents to Quinn and Claudia.

Sometimes I imagine what our lives would've been like if they hadn't died. I would have completed college. Maybe I would be a lawyer right now, like I wanted. I would have made smarter choices in my life if I knew I had my parents backing me up. I doubt I would have married Rob.

Maybe Quinn would have made better choices too.

Well, there's no point in debating what would've happened. They're dead, and there's nothing anyone can do about it.

CHAPTER 21

When I get back home, Rob is waiting for me in the kitchen. He's eating a bowl of cereal and he glares at me as I stomp the snow off my boots in the foyer, silently daring him to come yell at me. He doesn't.

"Where were you?" he asks as I walk into the living room in my bare feet.

"Just driving around, looking for Quinn."

He grunts. "You think you could find her better than the police?"

That's the problem with Rob. He never believes in me. A few years ago, I talked to him about the possibility of going back to college, or at least taking a few classes. *You're way too old for that, Claudia.* I hate to admit it, but his words got to me. I never ended up doing it.

"Maybe," I say.

"Well, did you?"

I roll my eyes. "No, I didn't."

He frowns. "You be careful, Claudia. You know, if you help her, you'll be aiding and abetting a criminal."

"Quinn isn't a criminal."

"She killed her husband. I would say that makes her a criminal."

"Watch it."

Our eyes meet across the table. I see a muscle twitch in Rob's jaw. Finally, he drops his eyes.

"If you're going to take my truck," he mutters, "at least let me know first."

"I wasn't gone long."

"Yeah, but I got a job to do, Claudia."

I snort. "What? Unclogging someone's toilet?"

He stands up so quickly, he nearly knocks his chair down. "Guess that's not as important as giving somebody a back rub, huh?"

I open my mouth to reply, but Rob has already brushed past me. He grabs his coat and his car keys, then he's out the door. The entire house shakes on its foundation when he slams the door shut.

I don't expect to go out again today anyway. I got rid of the phone. Presumably, the phone is currently making its way to Vermont. Nowhere near us. By the time the police track it down, Quinn will have had time to get even further away from here.

And when she calls me to tell me where she is—and I'm sure she will—I'm going to be ready.

———

I had a couple of massage clients scheduled in the afternoon, but everyone canceled because of the snow. It means I end up sitting around the house, worrying about what's happening with my sister. I also do a bit of laundry. Rob never, ever does laundry. He would keep buying underwear for months to avoid doing a load.

I call the police station and leave a message for Scott, but I don't get a call back until nearly five o'clock in the afternoon, while I'm sitting on my sofa, watching television to take my mind off of everything. Rob got called out on a job, and he took his truck with him.

"Did you find her?" I ask Scott, before he can get a word in.

His voice is gruff. "Not yet."

I allow my shoulders to relax. Of course they didn't find her. This guy is a small-town police deputy for a reason. He doesn't know how to investigate a murder. He has no idea how to find a person on the run. Maybe if the chief were here, they would have a chance.

"But it's just a matter of time," he adds. There's an ominous tone to his voice.

"What do you mean?"

"I mean we've got some leads."

"Did you find her phone?"

Scott hesitates. "We tracked it to Vermont, and I've got an officer going over there. But we have reason to believe she's still in the state. I don't think she's gone far."

I get a queasy feeling in my stomach. I thought dumping that cell phone in the car at the cemetery would send Scott on a wild goose chase that would give my sister at least another day of leeway. But it turns out he's smarter than I gave him credit for.

"Why do you say that?" I ask carefully.

"We found out she got pulled over last night on I-93 North, just before the state line. They didn't issue a ticket or anything like that, but she had a blown out tail light. The officer told her she had to get off the road, and he said he didn't see her again, so he assumed she did."

Oh Quinn, how could you be so stupid? I chew on my thumbnail. "But that was last night. She could be hundreds of miles away by now."

"Maybe. But there was a blizzard going on and she was in a compact car. She probably had to get off the road anyway, even without the tail light issue. And wherever she pulled over, she may very well be stuck. Anyway, we're checking it out."

I cringe. If she's still in New Hampshire, they'll find her soon. How did she not even manage to make it out of the state? I can get out of the state in less than two hours.

Of course, in the weather we were having last night,

without all-wheel drive or snow tires, she would've had to go pretty slowly. Still.

"Scott," I say, "you… you don't think Quinn killed her husband, do you?"

There's a long silence on the other line. "I'm not sure what to think right now. But it isn't looking good for her, Claudia. She left him lying dead in her house. And there was nobody else in the car with her when she got pulled over. It's not like somebody was holding a gun to her head."

I clench my right hand into a fist. "You *know* her though. You know she wouldn't do something like this."

"I don't know her."

I'm surprised how cold Scott's voice sounds. He dated Quinn. He was so infatuated with her. I could see it all over his face. And when she moved back here, I ran into him on the street and he started asking me all kinds of questions about her.

"What are you talking about?" I say. "She was your *girlfriend*."

"We dated for a few months ten years ago."

"She was your girlfriend. I know you cared about her a lot."

"That was a very long time ago." He pauses. "We were just kids then. It was nothing. I don't know her anymore—you know she keeps to herself."

He's not wrong about that. Derek and Quinn almost never entertained guests. My sister used to be outgoing, but after she got married, she turned into a hermit.

Scott lets out a sigh. "Claudia, I have to go. If you hear anything from Quinn, let me know right away."

"Will you tell me if you think you know where she is?"

"Yes."

But he hesitates for several seconds before answering, which makes me think he has absolutely no intention of telling me anything. Why should he? He doesn't want me to tip her off, after all.

Deputy Dwyer may be a better police officer than I gave him credit for. Although I still can't believe he didn't go into her house yesterday after he got the call about the screams.

After I hang up with Scott, I can't stop pacing across the living room. I was trying to give my sister a clear shot to escape the police, figuring she would contact me when they stopped looking for her, but it's not working. How did she manage to get herself pulled over? What was she doing with a blown out tail light anyway?

That's when I make a split second decision:

I'm going to look for her.

This is New England—the main roads will be clear by now. I need to find her before the police do. I have a sense of where they pulled her over. And I know Quinn better than anyone in the world.

I'm going to find my sister.

CHAPTER 22

It's dark by the time I get on the road. Fortunately, the snow has been cleared from the streets, so the tires don't slip too badly. I can only imagine Quinn taking this route last night, when the snow was really coming down. She didn't have a chance.

I merge onto the highway and start driving north. I filled up my tank in anticipation of the storm, so I've got enough gas to get me well across state lines, but I don't think I'll need to go that far.

Only a day earlier, Quinn took this exact route in her attempt to escape. I imagine her gripping the steering wheel, her eyes pinned down the road. I'm the one who taught Quinn to drive. She was very responsible about it. She would sit in the driver's seat, holding the wheel carefully in the nine and three positions, her shoulders stiff as a board. She passed the driving test on her first try, and the first thing she did was hug me.

I can find her. I know I can.

About an hour after I get on the road, my phone rings. I rifle around in my purse, searching for it with my fingers, but the first thing they come in contact with is the pocket knife. It's Rob's knife, which he uses when he goes fishing, but I borrowed it. I thought it would be a good idea to have a little protection handy. Just in case.

My fingers finally locate my phone. I pull it out of my purse without taking my eyes off the road. I glance down at the name on the screen.

It's the police station.

I put the phone on speaker and drop it into the cupholder. "Hello?" I say.

"Claudia? It's Deputy Dwyer."

"Hi, Scotty."

There's a pause in the other line. I wonder if I finally got to him by using his old nickname. "Listen, Claudia. Where are you?"

I freeze. "I'm… at home."

"No, you're not. I was just at your house and your husband told me you weren't home. He said he hasn't seen you since the morning and didn't know where you are."

"Oh…"

"Have you spoken to your husband recently?"

"No, I don't generally get his permission when I leave the house."

Scott ignores my jab. "So where are you then?

There's no way I can tell him where I really am. "I just stepped out for a bit. To the grocery store."

"I see." He doesn't sound like he believes me, but what can he do? Arrest me for not being home? "I'd be happy to meet you wherever you are. I'd like to speak to you."

A shiver runs down my spine. "About what?"

Another silence on the other line. "I'd rather talk in person. Where are you?"

I press my foot down on the gas, my head whipping back as the car accelerates. "Did you find Quinn?"

"No. Not yet."

I don't understand why he wants to speak to me so badly. And I don't like the idea of meeting him somewhere that isn't the police station. Not for the first time since I discovered my brother-in-law's dead body, I don't entirely trust Deputy Scott Dwyer.

"Claudia—"

"I'll let you know when I get home from the grocery store," I say.

Before he can say another word, I hang up the phone. There's an uneasy feeling in the pit of my stomach. What does Scott want to talk to me about? What was such a secret that he couldn't tell me about it on the phone?

It doesn't matter though. I'm not turning around and heading back home. I've come this far. I'm going to keep pushing forward.

An hour later, I'm getting close to the end of New Hampshire. This is where Quinn must've been when the police officer pulled her over for the broken tail light. I keep my eyes peeled for any area she might have pulled her car into. Now that the sun is down, any liquid left on the road is starting to freeze. I have to slow down to keep my wheels from slipping.

There's no way she could've gone much further than this in a snowstorm.

And that's when I see it. The tiny faded sign that I almost miss, but just barely catch.

Baxter Motel.

I don't know why, but my gut is telling me this is where Quinn ended up. She would have been looking for something small and out-of-the-way. And this is around where she got pulled over, so she knew she had to get off the road.

As I turn off the highway, following an equally faded sign pointing in the direction of the hotel, I pass a police car going in the opposite direction. It looks like they had the same idea I did. I slow down as much as I can and catch a glimpse of the backseat of the car. It's empty.

So they didn't find Quinn at the Baxter Motel.

I pull over on the side of the road, debating what to do next. The police obviously searched the motel and didn't find her there. Am I wasting my time?

But I still have that feeling. I think she would have

stopped here.

I'm going to check it out.

CHAPTER 23

The Baxter Motel is about what I might have expected from an out-of-the-way motel at a nearly nonexistent rest stop. It's decrepit, with the sign peeling and almost rotting, abutted by an equally decrepit house and what looks like it used to be a restaurant—now abandoned. If Quinn wanted a place to sleep for the night, and didn't want to sleep in her freezing car, this would be a perfect place to hide out.

The light is on in the motel's lobby. I step inside, and the first thing I see is a bucket in the center of the room, with water leaking down into it from the ceiling. There's a desk at the far end, and a man is sitting at a desk, looking down at his phone. But when he sees me walk in, he sits up rigidly.

I approach the desk tentatively. The guy sitting at the desk reminds me of the boys Quinn used to date in high school and college. He has those boy-next-door type of good looks, like Scotty Dwyer. That was her type—much more so than classically handsome Derek. I was always surprised she fell for Derek.

The man doesn't return my smile. His brown eyes are wary as they rake over me. I wonder if he recognizes me—people say Quinn and I have a resemblance although less so since she started dyeing her hair. "Yes?" he says.

He looks suspicious of me and I haven't even opened my mouth. Right off the bat, I sense I won't get much out of this guy. I have to try something else.

"Do you have any rooms for the night?" I ask.

He narrows his eyes at me. "A room?"

I blink at him. "This is a motel, isn't it?"

He looks at me for a long time, and he nods. "Yes. It's fifty dollars a night."

"Cash okay?"

"Yeah, fine."

He stands there, waiting while I fish around in my purse for my wallet. I pull out a twenty, two tens, and a five. I've got another three dollar bills, and now I'm counting change out.

"Fine," he says after I've counted out almost a dollar in change. "That'll do."

I let out a breath. I thought he was going to turn me away for being fifty cents short. "Thanks."

"I have to go change the sheets on the bed." He reaches

under the table and pulls out a yellowing sheet of paper. "I need you to fill this out for me."

It's the standard information sheet. Name, contact information, address. I'll have to make it all up.

The man ambles off, presumably to change the sheets on the bed, even though it's unnecessary. I'm not going to spend the night here. I'm only going to stay long enough to get the information I need.

I make up a fake name, and scribble in some fake address in my most illegible handwriting. My name is Melissa Smith and I live in Jefferson, New Hampshire.

While I'm waiting for the man to return, I get out my cell phone. There's another missed call from the police station. I don't call Scott back. Not now, anyway. Maybe after I get back home.

Idly, I type into the search engine on my phone: Baxter Motel New Hampshire.

I didn't expect to get any hits. Maybe a Facebook page with a link to a website "under construction." But instead, my entire screen fills with stories about the Baxter Motel. And the one word present in every single result is "murder." My heart jumps in my chest.

"All set, ma'am."

I jerk my eyes up from my phone screen. That man is standing in front of me, even though I didn't see him come back downstairs. I shove my phone back in my purse. Part of me wants to ask him if he knows that every single mention of his hotel on the Internet has the word "murder" in it. I have a feeling he does.

I swallow. "Thanks."

He grabs the sheet of paper that I just got done filling out. He scans my details and rolls his eyes.

"What?" I say.

"Nothing."

"You just rolled your eyes."

He puts down the piece of paper on the desk. "You really want to have this conversation?"

"What conversation?"

"Your information is fake." He shrugs. "It's fine."

I fold my arms across my chest. "What makes you so sure of that?"

"I used to live in Jefferson. You got the zip code wrong. Way off."

I open my mouth, not sure how to respond to that. "I…"

"I said it's fine." He waves to indicate I should follow him. "Come on upstairs, *Melissa*. I'm Nick, by the way."

I follow Nick up the stairs to the second floor. This motel could definitely use a new paint job, and it's almost frightening how much the stairs creak as I walk up them. This motel could use a new *everything*.

We pass rooms 201 and 202, and then we come to a stop in front of room 203. The door is still slightly open from when he must have changed the sheets. He drops the key into my hand. "Here you go."

I glance over his shoulder, into the tiny furnished motel room. At the hard bed and the tiny TV, and the small window. "Do you have anything for dinner here?"

He shoots me an irritated look. "I can make you a sandwich."

"Is it included with the price of the room?"

"I suppose it will have to be, since you didn't even have enough money to pay for the room."

I look down the hallway behind him, at the two closed doors. Rooms 201 and 202. Is it possible that my sister occupied one of those rooms? It's time to find out. "Is anyone else staying here?"

He raises his eyebrows at me. "I respect *your* privacy. Maybe you could respect the privacy of the other people staying here."

With those words, he turns and leaves me.

Wow, that guy really didn't like me. I'm not sure why, because he seemed belligerent from the second I came into the hotel. Maybe it's not me. Maybe he's having a bad night.

I enter the tiny motel room and shut the door behind me. I turn the lock, but then I notice a deadbolt as well. I swing it into place.

The double bed is just as uncomfortable as it looks. I shrug off my coat and settle down onto it, and a spring jabs me in the butt. I adjust the pillows behind my back so I can sit up, but these pillows have seen better days. There are three of them, and they're all flat as a pancake.

My phone rings. I reach into my purse to pull it out, and Rob's name is flashing on the screen. Undoubtedly, he's wondering where I am. If I tell him I went off looking for Quinn, he's not going to be thrilled. But I have to tell him something.

I take the call, and immediately, I hear crackling on the other line. "Claudia?"

"Hi, Rob," I say. "Listen, I'm sorry about taking off. There's just… There's somewhere I had to go…"

"Claudia, I…….." There's a good five seconds of nothing but crackling. "What……. can't hear……."

"I'm looking for Quinn," I say. "I'll be back late tonight. I promise."

There's more crackling, and then the line goes dead. I guess the reception is still bad after the storm. Oh well. I answered the phone, so at least he knows I'm not dead.

I settle down on the bed, and bring up the Internet browser on my phone. Now that I have some privacy, I can read about the Baxter Motel.

I click on the first link, which is an article from two years ago. The headline jumps out at me: *Woman Found Murdered in New Hampshire Motel.* The woman in question was twenty-five-year-old Christina Marsh. She was discovered dead in one of the motel rooms. Stabbed to death. There were no signs of forced entry.

The article notes that the owners of the hotel, Nicholas

and Rosalie Baxter, were working with the police to find the perpetrator.

I read the articles one by one, and the story materializes. The woman, Christina Marsh, had been staying at the hotel for about a week. She hadn't left her room in a day, so Nick Baxter went to check on her. He discovered her lying dead in a pool of her own blood.

Several of the articles mentioned a "relationship" between Nick Baxter and Christina Marsh. One went so far as to call her his girlfriend and implied the affair had been going on throughout her stay at the motel.

He was never charged with anything, at least not according to any of the articles. And I would assume if he had been convicted of murder two years ago, he wouldn't still be working here. So I'm guessing he was cleared.

I look down at the bedspread underneath me. Did it happen here? Was she killed in this very room?

I shove my phone into my purse. I'm supposed to be focused on Quinn, but something about this place makes me feel very uneasy. I need to do what I came here to do and get out.

I crack open the door to the hotel room. The hallway is empty. Quiet. I slip into the hall and look at the other two rooms. 201 and 202. This motel isn't much bigger than my house.

I try room 201 first. There's a "DO NOT DISTURB" sign hanging from the doorknob, but I ignore it as I rap my fist gently against the door. No answer. Then I knock again. Harder.

Nothing.

Then I try the doorknob. Locked.

I feel this crawling sensation on the back of my neck. I whirl around, just in time to catch somebody staring at me from room 202. A watery blue eye. Some silver hair.

Having been caught, I panic and scurry back into room 203. I close the door behind me and throw the deadbolt into place.

My mind is racing. Room 201 is obviously empty. Room 202 has a guest in it, so Quinn could never have been staying there. That means I should get back on the road.

I'll just wait a bit longer. To give myself more space between me and the police.

I figure I'll watch some TV, but I don't see the remote control anywhere. My eyes fall on the dresser next to the bed. Maybe the remote control is in the drawer. But I open it up and all I see in there is a copy of the Bible. Then as the drawer shifts, I see a spark of something shiny from underneath the Bible.

I push the Bible aside and that's when I see it. A wedding band.

My hands are trembling as I pull a gold wedding band out from the drawer. It looks like the one that my sister wore for the last two years. But there's only one way to be sure.

I tilt the band to the side and look on the inside. Wrapped around the inside of the band, I see the engraved letters: DEREK + QUINN.

Quinn was *here*. In this very room.

I lift my eyes, which make contact with the window. There's a house overlooking the motel. A rickety old two-story house. And there's a light on in one of the second-story windows. I can make out a silhouette of a woman sitting in front of the window.

Watching.

I shiver and almost drop the wedding band. The sight of this woman staring out the window has unnerved me. I look down at the wedding band in my hand. I need to get the hell out of here.

No. Not yet.

And then I hear a single knock at the door.

CHAPTER 24

The sound of the knock makes me nearly jump out of my skin. I just stand there for a moment, unsure what to do. I don't really want to open the door right now.

But maybe it's Nick with my dinner. I should check.

My phone buzzes on top of my bed. I glance over at the screen. It's the police station again. I let it go to voicemail.

After another moment of hesitation, I pull the door open. I almost gasp with relief when I see there's no one there. I look down—a plate containing a sandwich is lying on the ground. The sandwich has been hastily assembled— the top slice of bread is barely on top of the sandwich. I pick up the plate and examine my dinner. It is a turkey sandwich, nothing more and nothing less. No mayonnaise, no lettuce, no tomatoes. Just dry turkey and bread.

But it's free. Beggars can't be choosers.

Then again, I wonder if it's safe to eat. This guy who owns the motel, Nick Baxter, may very well be a cold-blooded killer. And it's clear he doesn't think much of me. Maybe I shouldn't be eating anything he gave to me.

I raise my eyes, and that's when I notice the door to room 202 has cracked open again. It's open just enough that both watery blue eyes stare out at me. She startled me before, but now I'm ready for her.

"Can I help you?" I say.

The door swings open further. Now I can see that the blue eyes belong to an elderly woman. She has long white hair and a deeply creased face. When she speaks, her voice is like sandpaper. "You are feistier than the other one."

I suck in a breath. This woman saw my sister here. Maybe they even talked. I drop the plate on a dresser inside my room and step into the hallway. "What other one?"

Her ancient lips curl into a smile.

"What other one?" I say, louder this time.

And then she slams the door in my face.

Great.

I want to say to hell with her and get out of here, but I can't do that. Quinn was here. I have a feeling Quinn spoke with this woman, and maybe this woman knows something. I've got to talk to her and figure out what she knows. Then I can leave.

I grab my purse and step across the hallway. I knock firmly on the woman's door. There's only silence on the other side. So I knock again.

"Excuse me?" I say. "I'd like to speak to you."

Silence.

"Please." I bring my face closer to the door. "Listen, the truth is... I'm looking for my sister. I think she was here. Can you help me?"

The silence behind the door is endless. Finally, I hear locks clicking open. The door creaks as loudly as the stairs as it swings open. The woman is standing there in a long, white nightgown, peering up at me.

"You say you are looking for her?" she asks me.

I squeeze my hands together. "I want to know what happened after she left the motel."

"Do you?"

I nod. "Can I come in?"

Her eyes narrow at me for a moment, but then she steps aside. My heart is racing, telling me this is a mistake, but I keep moving. I enter the old woman's room and allow her to lock the door behind me.

CHAPTER 25

This room is nothing short of terrifying.

It's all the mirrors. It's likely about the same size as my room, but mirrors cover every inch of the walls. It's like I'm in a fun house. I'm afraid I'm going to walk into the wall without realizing it, especially considering how dark it is in here.

"My name is Greta," the old woman tells me, fixing her blue eyes on me. For the first time, I notice she has an accent. Something East European.

"I'm Melissa," I say.

Her eyes darken. "We tell the truth in this room. Or else you leave."

She looks like she means it. I clear my throat. "Fine. I'm Claudia."

Greta gestures at her bed, and I sit gingerly on the

edge, clutching my purse to my chest. She sits beside me, her eyes luminous in the yellow light of the room. "She was here. Your sister, Quinn. Right where you are sitting."

"When?"

"Only hours ago."

I run my fingers along the sheets, as if I could almost touch her presence. "You spoke with her then?"

"Yes. And so did Nick. The police were here looking for her, and Nick lied to them. For her."

I was wondering why the police drove past me without having discovered Quinn here, when they obviously had been looking. Now it all makes sense. That guy Nick lied to them. No wonder he was so squirrely when I came in. "That was nice of him."

"It was. But Rosalie did not like it."

"Who is Rosalie?" The name sounds strangely familiar, like one I heard recently.

She smiles thinly. "She is his wife."

Right. That's where I know the name. I saw it in all those articles. Rosalie Baxter. The co-owner of the motel. The one whose husband cheated on her and then his mistress ended up dead.

"Is Rosalie here?" I ask.

Greta shakes her head. "She does not leave her home. She is always at the window. She is always watching."

I shiver, remembering the silhouette of that woman in the window of the house next door. "Do you know what happened to my sister?"

Greta is silent for a moment, as if debating what to say next. "She did not leave."

"So is she still here? Is she in room 201?"

"I did not say she is still here. I just said she did not leave."

This is like one of those ridiculous riddles, like what goes up and down without moving? (The stairs.) "What do you mean?"

"I think you know what I mean."

I shake my head, my stomach sinking.

Greta stands up from the bed. She's so tiny, yet somehow her presence fills the room. There's something about her. "I read your sister's fortune," she says. "It was very dark. Her past was dark, and her future was even darker."

"Dark?"

She turns to look into one of the mirrors. Her reflection stares back at me. "I'm talking about *death*, Claudia. There was a death in her past and death in her future. And the worst part…"

I hold my breath. "What?"

"It was emanating from her." Greta's voice is a hiss. "Like a stench. Or a *virus*. Infecting everyone around her."

This woman seems like a crackpot, but there's something about her. She *knows* something. "How do you know my sister didn't leave?"

She turns to look directly at me. "Go outside. Go to Rosalie's."

"Rosalie's *what*?"

"Not what. *Where*. To Rosalie's."

I frown. "You mean to the house?"

"No. Not the house."

"But—"

"Go." She holds up her wrinkled hand. "I have told you all I know."

"Have you?"

She just stares at me, her chest rising and falling under her nightgown.

I rise from the bed. "Because I'm not sure you have."

"Go," she says, more firmly this time.

Maybe she does know more, but it's clear she has no intention of sharing it with me. Whatever I'm looking for is outside of this motel. And I'm going to find it.

———

I take my purse and my coat with me when I leave my room. I also keep Quinn's wedding band tucked away in my pocket. I have no intention of coming back here. The police are long gone—it's time to get on the road as soon as I'm done here.

Just as I'm going down the hall, I run into that guy Nick. He's got a tool kit in his hand, and he almost drops it.

"Hi," I say. "I'm, uh…" Somehow I don't want to tell

him I'm leaving. Not yet.

Nick nods at room 201. "Going to fix that leak."

"Good luck," I say.

He grunts.

When I get back down into the lobby, it's eerily empty. The ceiling is still leaking into that bucket. Every time there's a drip of water, I hear a noise. Plunk plunk plunk. Good thing he's getting that fixed. It's going to destroy the ceiling. Rob always talks about how people don't call him fast enough for a leak, and then they wreck the ceiling. He can fix the leak, but he can't fix that.

But that's not my problem. Quinn is my only problem.

I drop the keys to my room on the desk, next to where he left his cell phone behind—he's awfully trusting to leave that sitting there. Anyway, he'll get the idea that I left. That's fifty bucks down the drain. Well, forty-eight bucks.

When I get out of the motel, the temperature is about twenty degrees colder than it was when I first came in. The wind hits me in the face, and I regret not having brought a scarf. What's wrong with me? I've lived in New Hampshire my whole life. I know how cold it gets.

Rosalie's. *Find Rosalie's.*

Rosalie's *what*? What the hell was that old woman talking about?

I scan the outside of the hotel. I parked my car all the way in the back of the lot. I look up and see the old house next to the motel. That one light on the second floor that's still on. And the silhouette is still in the window, like she hasn't moved one inch since the last time I looked.

Is that Rosalie? Is she watching me?

I swivel my head to the other side, to check out that old abandoned building. It looks like it used to be a restaurant, but now it's all boarded up. I squint into the darkness, and I can just make out a sign on the restaurant that is caked in dirt and snow. I can't quite see what it says.

I trudge through the snow to get a closer look. It's only when I'm a stone throw away that I can see the writing, but I still can't make it out. I've got to get a little closer.

I inch forward on the ground, which is now lined with ice. I don't want to slip and break my wrist, but I need to see what the sign says. It isn't until I'm about six feet away that I can finally read the writing.

Rosalie's.

I shiver and hug my purse. This is the place Greta was talking about. Did Quinn go inside?

I make my way over to the front door of the abandoned restaurant. The door is not just closed, but boarded up. I cup my hands around my eyes, squinting to see inside. But it's completely dark. There are no signs of movement.

But Greta said to come here. What was she talking about?

I walk around the side of Rosalie's. I'm going very slowly because of how slippery the ice is. I have to hold onto the side of the restaurant to keep from slipping. It isn't until

I get around the back that I see something blue peeking out from behind a garbage bin.

I hurry over, as fast as I dare. When I am about ten feet away, I can make it out clearly. It's a Corolla. Quinn's car.

That's what Greta was talking about. She knew Quinn wasn't at the motel anymore. But she knew she hadn't left because her car is still here. Although God knows how she knew the car was here, considering how well concealed it is. You can't see it from the motel.

I walk the rest of the way to the car. When I get over to the car, I grab onto it so as not to fall. I look inside, but unsurprisingly, the car is empty.

A gust of wind nearly knocks me off my feet. My eyes are tearing from the cold. Or maybe from something else.

I look up. I can still see that broken down old house with the one light on in the upstairs bedroom. From that house, you can see everything. You can see the parking lot of the motel. You can see Quinn's car behind the restaurant. And you can see through the window of room 203.

The police were here looking for her, and Nick lied to them. For her.

That was nice of him.

It was. But Rosalie did not like it.

Rosalie.

I've got to talk to her.

But one thing is for sure, I'm not going to end up like my sister. I'm smarter than that. I feel around in my purse until my fingers make contact with their destination: Rob's pocket knife.

My heart is pounding as I carefully walk the distance from the restaurant to the dilapidated old house, my boots crunching against the hardening snow. Even though the snow has stopped, the wind is brutal, like an ice cold dagger in my face. Every few seconds, I glance up at the second-floor window of the house. The light is still shining. Rosalie has not moved. Not a millimeter. She is still in the window, staring down at me. I squint up at her, trying to make out any features. But I can't.

My legs feel like rubber as I reach the small house. The door is made of wood, which has splintered over the years and nobody bothered to fix it. The paint surrounding the door is outright peeling off. Like our house, it's a fixer-upper that nobody bothered to fix.

I swallow a lump in my throat. Maybe this is a mistake. Maybe I should turn around and leave.

I feel the weight of the knife in my hand. It gives me confidence. I've never let anyone push me around. I can deal with one small woman.

Right?

I knock on the door with my left hand. There's no answer. Rosalie isn't coming down. I suppose I'm not surprised.

I put my hand on the door knob. I let out a gasp as it turns. The door is unlocked.

I push open the door and walk inside.

CHAPTER 26

ROSALIE

I'm not dead.

Did you think I was? That I'm some corpse my husband propped up in front of the second-floor window to frighten his guests?

I'm not. I'm very much alive.

And I'm afraid my husband is a murderer.

Twelve Years Earlier

I can hear the hum of the engine and my body jolts with every imperfection in the road. My teeth sink into my lower lip as I shift in the passenger seat of the broken down Ford. A blindfold covers my eyes, shrouding me in darkness.

I desperately claw at the blindfold with my right hand. Before I can work it loose, a powerful hand encircles my wrist. My boyfriend Nick's voice cuts through the silence. "Hey, quit doing that," he says.

I groan. "Nick…"

"I mean it. I want this to be a surprise. No peeking."

"Fine. How much longer?"

"Ten minutes—tops."

"At nine minutes and thirty seconds, I'm ripping this blindfold off. I swear, Nick."

I have been dating Nick Baxter for six years. We met in high school, if you can believe that. High school sweethearts—I know, I know. I never imagined meeting the love of my life in high school, but the second I kissed him at only sixteen years old, I just knew. This was the guy.

Have you ever just met somebody that you clicked with? That you felt was an extension of yourself? The missing piece. From the first moment we sat down to dinner on our first date, I felt like I could tell him anything. And I did. I told him I didn't want to be a teacher like my parents kept telling me to be. I wanted to be a chef. I wanted to open my own restaurant. It was my dream. I fell in love with him for being the only one to believe in me.

Also, it doesn't hurt that he's pretty hot. Even with my eyes blindfolded, I can picture his dark blond hair, his slim but muscular build, and his infectious smile. Girls always give Nick a second look, but he only has eyes for me. Whether I deserve it or not, he worships the ground I walk on.

I feel the car swerving to the right, which means he is exiting the highway. Thank God. If we don't get there soon, I swear I'm going to vomit. If that happens, he's going to have to clean it up all by himself, because this is his own damn fault.

The car jerks to a halt. Nick's warm, large hand squeezes my knee. I can imagine the eager look on his face. "Okay, Rosie. We're here."

"Can I take off the blindfold?"

"Give me one minute."

He insists on guiding me out of the car. He rests his hand on top of my head to make sure I don't bump my head on the door frame. He places his hands on my shoulders and turns me about ninety degrees. Then he yanks off the blindfold.

"Ta-da!" he says.

I blink, adjusting to the light. "Ta-da what?"

"It's your new restaurant."

My new *restaurant*? Is he *joking* with me?

I've been working as a line cook at a dingy restaurant since graduating culinary school. The salary is just barely enough that I could give up my waitressing job, since my parents have not given me one penny to subsidize my "ridiculous lifestyle." Nick recently graduated from college with a degree in business, and he's been talking about the two of us starting a restaurant. I said sure, figuring it was just a pipe dream.

And now we are standing in front of a one story building that looks like it should be condemned. All the windows are cracked, there's dirt ground into every single crack and crevice, and the door is literally hanging by one hinge. As I stare at the place, a rat scurries out the front door. I'm sure there are plenty more where that one came from.

This place is horrible. It is *not* a good surprise. I feel like the blindfold was unnecessary.

"Oh," I say. I'm trying to look happy, but it's straining my acting skills.

"I know it doesn't look great now," he says quickly. "But I got it dirt cheap. Trust me, Rosie, this is a great location. I scoped it out, and there are no restaurants along I-93 for twenty minutes in either direction."

"Mmm," I say.

"I'm going to help you get it cleaned up," he says, "and you'll see, this place is going to be a huge success. I promise."

"Mmm," I say again.

He looks me straight in the eyes. "This is your dream. I'm going to make it happen for you."

He sounds so sure of himself. I love Nick, but I think

he overextended himself with this one. But I'll go along with it. After all, what do I have to lose?

*

Nine Years Earlier

It feels decadent to be taking a day off.

It's all I do anymore. Work. The restaurant opens for lunch, and I'm usually there till it closes late in the evening. I recently hired help so that I could at least have one night off, only after Nick bugged me to do it. I don't trust anyone to do as good a job as I do, and also, I love being there. I love being in the kitchen of my own restaurant. It's everything I ever wanted.

But today I have a day off, and Nick persuaded me to go to a local carnival. We rode on the roller coaster, then on the Ferris wheel, and now we're sharing a giant blob of pink cotton candy.

"I forgot how good cotton candy is," Nick says as he stuffs a big fuzzy wad of it into his mouth. "You should serve this in the restaurant."

"Um, no."

"You should. It will probably become your bestselling dessert."

I give him the side eye. "I'm not even sure if you're kidding."

"I'm not!"

I'm still somewhat in disbelief over how successful our restaurant has become. I'm not going to lie—the first year was rough. It took forever to get Rosalie's cleaned up and in condition to serve as a restaurant. Nick and I worked our butts off. We replaced all the windows, cleaned everything out by hand, bought all new kitchen appliances and furniture for the dining area. We invested a lot of money and a lot of labor. And for the first few months, I thought it was all going to be for nothing. I could count on one hand the number of customers on a given week. There were about twenty times that first year when I thought about giving up.

I'm not sure what Nick did, but our business picked up at the end of that first year. We started getting steady customers, and the second year, we broke even. The third year, we turned a profit.

Then a few months ago, Nick bought the two houses next door. One for us to live in and the other to turn into a motel.

So we're going to buy a house together? I said when he told me his plans. *That sounds pretty serious. We're not even married.*

Well, we should probably do something about that, he said.

The bastard had a ring in his pocket. I said yes. Obviously. I couldn't imagine spending my life with anyone else.

We're getting married next month. It will be a small ceremony at City Hall—just close family. Mostly because all of our money has been sunk into the restaurant and the new motel. And also, neither of us have big families. Plus, my parents don't like Nick. My mother is never clear about why, but she always hints that I could do better, and she doesn't think much of our restaurant either. That's why I don't speak to her much anymore. I'm not even sure she's coming to the wedding.

"I'll let the cotton candy idea percolate," Nick says. "In the meantime, what do you want to ride next? Should we ride that one that turns you around in a circle in the air and then upside down?"

I look at the ride he's pointing to. Just the sight of it makes my stomach turn. "No, thank you. How about…" I look over at a little black tent with the sign on the front with painted black lettering that reads, *Fortune-telling, three tickets.* "Ooh, I want to get my fortune told!"

Nick snorts. "You don't need to go to a fortuneteller to know your fortune. I can tell it to you right now." He presses his fingertips into his temples. "The future is saying you're going to marry a super handsome business genius, and then you're going to have five kids together."

"Hmm. Are you sure the future is saying five kids? Because I'm kind of feeling like it might be three."

"Pretty sure it's five."

We have always talked about having kids in an abstract sort of way, but now that we're actually getting married, these talks have become a little more serious. We both want a lot of kids. We're both only children, and we've always wanted big families. But five seems like an awful lot. And he's not the one who has to push them out.

"See," I say, "this is why I need to talk to the fortuneteller. And in the meantime, you can try to win me a decent prize this time."

Earlier in the day, Nick played a game where he had to knock down bottles with a ball. He did spectacularly badly and insisted the game was rigged. Anyway, he won me a tiny rubber duck, which wasn't really worth carrying around, so I tossed it.

Nick salutes. "You got it. I'm winning you a stuffed animal so big, one of us will have to ride on top of the hood on the way home."

That remains to be seen.

While Nick goes to find his game of choice, I walk toward the black tent. I've never had my fortune told before, but it always seemed like fun. I don't believe in stuff like that, but there's no harm in it.

The curtains of the tent are slightly parted, and I push them aside with my hand and peek my head in. The tent is lit by only a few candles, but it's enough to see the contents. There's a small wooden table inside, and a folding chair on either side of it. On one of the two chairs sits a woman with long black hair. And by black, I mean *black*. I've heard black described as the absence of color, but I never understood that description until I saw this woman's hair.

She raises her eyes to look at me, and they're just as black as her hair. So black that I could not possibly see her pupils. "Hello," she says.

"Hi." My voice cracks unexpectedly and I clear my throat. "You do… fortune-telling?"

She nods and gestures at the folding chair across from her. "Please have a seat."

I hand over my three tickets, which she stuffs into the purple robe she's wearing. I study her features, partially obscured by the shadows. I can't tell how old she is. She could be twenty or she could be sixty. It's so strange.

"My name is Naomi," she says.

"I'm Rosalie."

"That's a pretty name." Her black eyes flit down to my left hand. "And that's a pretty ring."

I squeeze my left hand into a fist subconsciously. The diamond is tiny—all we could afford—but I love it. "Yes. Thank you."

"He is a good man." She says it like it isn't a question. "At least, you believe he is a good man."

"He is," I say, with fierce loyalty.

Something almost resembling a smile touches Naomi's lips. "We shall see."

She picks up a deck of Tarot cards. I've seen Tarot

cards before, but I've never had my fortune read before. I know the whole thing is silly, but my stomach churns. I wish I had stayed outside and cheered Nick on while he won me another prize (or failed to win me another prize).

She lays three cards out on the table. She stares down at the cards for a moment, her fingers lingering on the middle card, which is a tower on fire after being struck by lightning, with two men hurling downward to their death. I know nothing about Tarot cards, but this doesn't look good.

"What?" I say.

"This is The Tower," she says. "It means you will have a life altering revelation. One that will leave you blindsided."

I shake my head. "Like what?"

Maybe I'm pregnant. My period isn't due till next week, but I forgot to take my pill a couple of nights this month. Nick would love that.

Naomi touches the rightmost card. This one is even more disturbing. It's a picture of a knight riding a horse with a dead person below the horse's feet. Except the knight's helmet is raised and you can see it is actually a skeleton. I can make out the word on the card.

Death.

Naomi raises her eyes sharply. She reaches out and grabs my wrist with fingers that are as cold as the skeleton on the card.

"Rosalie," she hisses. "You must not marry that man."

"*What?*" I try to yank my hand away, but she's holding on tight. "What are you talking about?"

"Please." Her black eyes lock with mine. "You must listen to me. You think this man will bring you happiness, but he won't. He will bring death into your life."

"Death?" I repeat. "You mean… he's going to *die*?"

The thought of Nick dying is like a hand squeezing my heart. I can't imagine my life without him.

"No," she says firmly. "He will not die. He will bring the death of another."

"You mean…" My head is spinning. "He's going to kill someone?"

She is silent. She releases my hand, but I'm too stunned to move.

"*God.*" I shake my head. This is preposterous. I don't believe in this stuff, but there's something about this woman… "You don't know Nick. He's a good guy. And he is… He would *never* hurt anyone. Ever. And… I love him. A *lot.*"

"But that will change."

"No, it *won't.*" I glare down at the cards in front of her. "So basically, you flip over a tower and a skeleton, and then you say that my fiancé is a murderer? This is the most ridiculous thing I've ever heard."

"It is not just the picture on the card." Her voice is quiet. "It is what the cards say to me. This is the gift I have."

She frowns at me. "You still have time. You can call it off."

I open my mouth to tell her off, to say that there is no way in hell I would ever break up with the man I love because of some psychic at a stupid carnival. But somehow, no words come out.

"Think about it, Rosalie," she says. "I can only show you the right path. You must choose to walk it."

My hands are shaking when I get out of the psychic's tent. It was so dark in there that the sunlight startles me. I blink a few times as my eyes adjust.

"I did it!"

I turn around and find Nick holding up a stuffed panda triumphantly. It's about a foot tall, so not so big that it won't fit in the backseat, but admittedly more impressive than that rubber duck. He has an adorably proud grin on his face, and I throw my arms around his neck. And I can't seem to let go.

"Whoa!" He laughs. "I didn't know you were such a fan of pandas."

But when I pull away from him, the smile drops off his face. It's only then that I realize there are tears streaking down my cheeks.

"Rosie, what's wrong?" he asks. "Are you okay?"

I blink back fresh tears. "I'm fine."

"You're *not* fine." He glances at the black tent. "What the hell happened in there?"

"She…" I take a shaky breath. I hadn't meant to tell

him what Naomi said to me or let it ruin my day, but I can't help myself. "She told me something bad would happen if we got married. That we should call off the wedding."

His mouth drops open. "Are you *kidding* me? She said that to you?"

I nod slowly.

He shoves the panda into my hands. "That is unacceptable. I'm going to go talk to her."

I grab his arm. "Nick, please don't."

"But she upset you!" A muscle twitches in his jaw. "She has some nerve. She's just some cheap carnival fake psychic. You know nothing she says is real. Right? It's all just a show."

"Right…"

"Rosie…" His brown eyes are wide. "You're not really taking this seriously, right? She's not psychic. That's not even a real thing."

"I know."

"And… I love you." He reaches out and grabs my hand in his. "If we didn't get married, I don't know what I would do. There's no one else I would ever want to spend my life with."

I swallow down a lump in my throat. "I love you too."

"I mean," he says. "That psychic said something bad would happen if we got married, but I honestly can't imagine anything worse than not being with you."

I feel the same way. "I know."

"So…" One side of his lips quirks up. "You won't break up with me because of what that psychic said?"

I allow myself a teeny tiny smile. "I guess not."

He kisses me, squishing the stuffed panda between us. I try to enjoy it, but I can't quite push away what that psychic told me. I don't believe in this stuff—I know it's fake. But I can't stop seeing the frightened look in her eyes.

CHAPTER 27

Six Years Earlier

You don't even realize you have everything until your whole life falls apart.

I've been married to Nick for three years now. I married him as planned, despite the psychic's warning. And surprise, surprise—nothing horrible happened. Nick never murdered anyone. He's been a pretty great husband, all things considered. And for a long time, our lives were good. Rosalie's is thriving, and even the motel is turning a nice profit. We were fixing up the house we live in—a monster job—but we got sidetracked because...

I got pregnant.

We were waiting for our businesses to be a bit more

stable and to finish our renovation work on the house, even though Nick was keen to get a move on and have our five babies. (Yeah, right.) Finally, he persuaded me to go off birth control, and on our very first try, we made a baby.

Then only two weeks after my positive pregnancy test, the bleeding started.

Nick took it worse than I did. He was so excited about starting a family, and he had already been suggesting terrible baby names. I was sad about it too, but I had read how common early pregnancy losses are, especially for a first pregnancy. I was sad, but I knew we would try again.

Then a week after my miscarriage, I woke up unable to feel my right foot.

Now it's four months later. I'm sitting in the office of a neurologist named Dr. Heller, a tall, thin woman with half-moon glasses that rest low on the bridge of her nose. She has two armchairs set up in front of her desk—Nick is sitting in one and I'm in the other. My cane is leaning against the desk, because I would fall if I tried to walk without it. And Dr. Heller has just uttered two words that will completely change my life.

"Multiple sclerosis?" Nick blurts out. His face looks how mine feels. "Are you sure?"

"Yes," she says simply. "Technically, you need to be having symptoms for a year to make this diagnosis, but I feel fairly certain. And unfortunately, you have a primary progressive form of the disease, since your neurological symptoms have gotten no better, even with the steroids, and have in fact progressed."

She's right. The symptoms have not gotten better—not even a little bit. They have *progressed*. The numbness has spread to my other foot.

"So what's the treatment?" he asks.

"With primary progressive multiple sclerosis, there's no proven treatment," she says. "We can try some medications, but…"

No treatment. There's nothing we can do. I will continue to *progress*.

Nick shakes his head. "I don't understand how this happened. She doesn't have any weird neurological diseases in her family."

"It doesn't always run in families," Dr. Heller says. "It's possible in your case, the pregnancy triggered it. And there's a chance that if you get pregnant again, your symptoms could get worse."

"A chance," he repeats. "So it's not for sure?"

"No," she says. "It's uncertain. Especially since Rosalie has a much less common form of the disease. But you should be aware of the possibility."

We return home after that appointment, both of us visibly shaken. Nick hardly says a word the entire drive home. That muscle twitches in his jaw the way it always does when he's upset. I spend most of the drive staring out the window, trying to figure out what's going to happen for the rest of my life.

The tower card. The life-altering revelation. Multiple sclerosis. The end of life as I know it.

It's come true.

When we walk into our house, I sit down at the kitchen table, but Nick just stands there. He doesn't say anything for several seconds, but it's obvious he has something to say. I look up at him, waiting. And then he says it.

"So it's just a *possibility*, right?" He folds his arms across his chest. "That doesn't mean if you get pregnant again, you're definitely going to get worse."

I knew that's what he was thinking. I knew it, but I wasn't sure if he would have the gall to say it. I mean, it's easy for him to be glib about it. He's not the one whose body is literally attacking itself.

I glare at him. "So you're okay with taking that chance?"

His face falls. "Rosie, you want a family too, don't you? I thought we were on the same page. Five kids, right?"

I can't even joke about it. There's nothing funny about what's happening to us right now. "I'm not willing to sacrifice everything for it though."

"Yes, but…" His voice drops. "Our family is everything too."

"So I'm not enough for you?"

"No. *No*." He pinches the bridge of his nose. "It's just… It's a lot to give up. You know?"

Of course I know. I've wanted to be a mother my whole life. But over the last four months, I've been learning how hard it is to walk without being able to feel my feet. If this gets worse, I don't know what will happen. I don't know how I'll be able to run the restaurant. And I certainly don't know how I'll be able to run after a bunch of kids.

"I'm sorry," I say. "I just can't risk it."

"But…"

"The answer is *no*, Nick. I won't change my mind."

He looks stricken. He collapses into a chair across from me. "Okay…"

There's a lump in my throat. He's right. It's a lot to give up. And he's always wanted to have kids so badly. It's not right to ask this of him.

"Listen…" I reach for his hand, and he gives it to me reluctantly. "I love you, but I understand if you want to… If this is too much for you. I would understand. We don't have to be together if you don't want to be anymore."

Nick jerks his head back. "What are you talking about? You think I want to break up?"

"I'm just saying. I would understand."

He squeezes my hand firmly in his. "Look, I'm not thrilled about this. Obviously. But I love you. And there's *nothing* that would make me not want to be with you anymore."

We sit there together in the kitchen for a long time, holding hands and contemplating what the rest of our lives will be like together. I have no idea at that moment how bad things are going to get.

Four Years Earlier

I hate the ceiling of our bedroom.

We had it painted when we moved in, but it's covered in cracks. Whoever painted it did a terrible job. The cracks are all over the place, forming spiderweb patterns in the white plaster. It needs to be redone, but let's face it, that's the least of our problems. It doesn't even make the top twenty.

"Rosie?"

I didn't even realize the sound of the shower had turned off. I shut my eyes, feeling that familiar wave of fatigue wash over me. I slept all night, but I'm still exhausted. When the alarm went off ten minutes ago, I woke up to shut it off, but I felt far from ready to get out of bed.

"Rosie?"

Nick is out of the shower. His dark blond hair looks even darker from the water, and he has a towel wrapped around his waist, revealing a pretty nice upper body. He looks really good. Every bit as handsome as the day I fell in love with him. Maybe more—he's grown up from that sixteen-year-old boy.

I don't want to think about what he must see when he looks at me now.

"Hey, Rosie," he says. "I got the bench set up in the shower for you if you want to go in."

He grabs my walker and brings it to the side of the bed. I never got pregnant again, but it didn't matter. My legs got weaker anyway, even faster than Dr. Heller predicted. I went from a cane to crutches, and now I use a walker most of the time. At my appointment last week, Dr. Heller wrote a prescription for a wheelchair.

I'm still working at the restaurant, but it's gotten very difficult. I'm struggling. It's not just that I'm having difficulty walking and getting around. My brain is muddled. I mix up orders and forget what I'm doing in the middle of doing it. It's embarrassing.

"Rosie? Do you need help sitting up?"

I stare at him. I have to get up and get to the restaurant. To my job that I *love*, that I dreamed of all my life. Except I just… don't want to. The idea of getting out of bed, taking a shower, getting dressed… even running a comb through my hair is so exhausting. I can't even contemplate it.

"I'm not getting up," I say.

He frowns. "Are you sick?"

He's so damn *nice* about everything. So willing to help me with every little thing. I used to love that about him. I never realized until recently how *annoying* it could be.

"Yes, I'm sick."

He sits down on the edge of the bed. He reaches for my forehead and I swat him away. "What's wrong?"

"I have multiple sclerosis."

He rolls his eyes. "Come on. Get up. There are going to be customers waiting outside."

"No."

"I don't understand."

"I don't want to work at the restaurant anymore."

He tries again to reach for me, but I shrug him off. "Is this about the kitchen being accessible? Because I told you, I called a contractor and got a quote—"

"I'm not going back to that restaurant," I say through my teeth. "Not now. Not ever."

"But—"

"I'm not going, Nick."

He gets up off the bed. "So what am I supposed to do?"

"There are other people who do the cooking. You can handle it."

He presses his lips together. "Fine. I'll take care of it today. You can have one sick day."

He throws off the towel and starts getting dressed. Once again, I can't help but think how attractive my husband is. But the scariest part is I feel nothing right now. Not even the slightest trace of desire. And I'm too tired to care.

CHAPTER 28

Three years earlier

As the credits roll on the television screen, I grab the remote control and flick to a new station. Somehow in the last six months, I've become the sort of woman who sits around the house all day, watching soap operas. It's literally the only thing that I do the entire day. Well, that's not true. In the morning, I watch game shows. And sometimes I surf the web on my phone. I occasionally eat a little. *Occasionally.* I've become skeletal.

Anyway, there's not much for me to do anymore. Rosalie's closed three months ago. It fell apart quickly after I stopped working there.

I hear Nick's heavy footsteps coming up to the second

floor. I glance down on my watch—it's the middle of the day. Sometimes he'll come home for lunch, but that was two hours ago. I wonder what he's doing home.

The thought of it makes me uneasy.

Nick appears at the bedroom door. There are faint purple circles under his eyes, but he manages a thin smile. He doesn't smile for real very much these days. That's fair though. He doesn't have a lot to smile about.

"Hi," I say.

He glances over my shoulder, at the bedroom window. "It's stuffy in here. You should open the window. It's a nice day outside."

"I'm fine."

But he still pushes past me and walks over to the window. I back up a few inches in my wheelchair. I use the chair all the time now. I gave up on walking several months ago, around when Rosalie's shut down. The amount of effort it takes to take a few steps isn't worth it.

Nick throws the window open. I suppose it's nice outside—the same cool spring day when Nick first took me out to see the restaurant all those years ago. But I've lost so much weight in the last two years that the breeze goes straight through me, and I shiver. Sometimes it feels like my skin is hanging off my bones.

"Better, right?" he says.

I nod, because it's easier than arguing. I'll close it again when he leaves.

"Maybe we could go outside together?" he says.

I cringe. "I don't want to deal with the stairs."

He blows out a breath. "You know, I can convert the dining room into a bedroom. I told you I could—"

"It's fine. I don't feel like going outside anyway."

Nick mumbles something under his breath that I can't make out. It's probably better I didn't hear it.

"What are you doing home?" I ask him.

He frowns and wrings his hands together. He's here for a reason. He didn't just come up here to open the window. He may as well spit it out already.

"Don't be mad," he says, "but I called Dr. Heller yesterday."

I look up at him sharply. Why would he call my neurologist without my permission? "Excuse me?"

"Look, you just seem…" He sinks down onto the bed so he can see eye to eye with me. "I'm *worried* about you, Rosie."

"So what *brilliant* insight did Dr. Heller have?"

He pushes on, ignoring my sarcasm. "She thought you should do a course of physical therapy."

"Physical therapy?"

He nods eagerly. "I'll take you to the appointments," he says. "Will you go, Rosie?"

"What's the point?" I say bitterly. "How am I supposed to walk better if I can barely move my legs?"

"Not for that," he says. "Dr. Heller said it would help

you get more independent, so I wouldn't have to—"

I glare at him. "Oh, I get it now. You're sick of helping me with every damn thing."

I shouldn't be surprised. Nick does a *lot* for me. He helps me in and out of bed—he even helps me into the shower and to get dressed in the morning. Even though I'm the chef in the family, he brings me all my meals now. He does everything for me. He never even complains. Not until now.

"Rosie, that's not—"

"Just admit it, Nick. It's not like anyone would blame you."

He hangs his head. "Don't do this. I'm just trying to help."

I study his face. "Did Dr. Heller have any other *helpful* advice?"

After an interminable pause, he digs into his pocket and pulls out a little orange bottle of pills. I inhale sharply.

"What's that?"

"They're antidepressants," he says. "Dr. Heller thought they might help."

"Oh God."

"Rosie…"

"I'm not taking those," I say. "I don't have depression. My situation is the problem. *Anyone* would be depressed in my situation."

"They still might help." He tries to reach for my hand,

but I pull away. "Please, Rosie. Just try it. For a few weeks. If you don't like it, you don't have to keep taking them. But maybe they'll help."

I look into his eyes. He still loves me, for some reason. He's just trying to help.

"Fine." I accept the bottle. "I'll try them for a few weeks."

But that night, I flush all the pills down the toilet.

———

Whenever I hear footsteps on the stairs, my heart leaps into my chest.

It's almost always Nick. Who else would it be, visiting me in the middle of the day? That butterflies sensation reminds me of when we were first dating, of how excited I used to be to see him.

Except that's not why I get butterflies now. I'm worried that any day now, Nick will throw up his hands. Tell me he's done with me. He's had enough.

It hasn't happened yet, but it will. A person can only take so much.

But this time, it's not Nick at all. It's the silver haired, elderly woman who has permanently moved into one of the rooms at the motel. Her name is Greta, and she and Nick struck up a deal for a reasonable monthly rate to allow her to live at the motel long term.

I like Greta—she's my only friend right now. She's

incredibly eccentric, with her long silver hair and her propensity to wear nightgowns twenty-four hours a day. But her visits to my room are the only bright spot in my week. She entertains me with stories about her life back in the carnival, or about her childhood back in Hungary. Or about Bernie, the carnie who used to be her husband before he dropped dead of a heart attack.

"Hello, Rosalie," she says in her East European accent.

"Hi, Greta."

She cocks her head to the side. "You need to eat more. Soon you will be so skinny, my bad eyes won't be able to see you anymore."

I laugh and tug subconsciously at my T-shirt, which was snug when I bought it five years ago, and now is swimming on me. "I'm fine."

"I will bring you food next time," she says. "Something I cooked myself. And you will eat every bite."

"Sure," I murmur.

She sits beside me—her on the bed and me in my wheelchair. Her eyes rake over me and I shift in my chair. "I don't like your aura today, Rosalie."

"Sorry?"

She frowns at me. "I will read your fortune today."

A sick sensation washes over me. I knew Greta used to tell fortunes in the carnival, but this is the first time she offered to tell my fortune. I never told her about that experience with Naomi, the woman who warned me about the terrible things that would happen if I married Nick.

She was right about the tragedy that changed my life. On the plus side, Nick hasn't murdered anyone. Not as far as I know, anyway.

"I'd rather you didn't," I say.

Greta clasps my hand in hers. It's cold and bony, the same as the fortune teller at the carnival all those years ago. "Tell me. What is your hesitation?"

"I just think... It's all sort of silly."

She studies my face. "No. You don't think it's silly. You are afraid."

I swallow, my mouth suddenly bone dry. "I had my fortune told a long time ago and it didn't go well."

Greta's eyes widen. "Tell me what happened."

I realize I haven't told anyone about that day at the carnival. I told Nick part of it, but not the entire story. I have carried it alone all these years.

"She predicted my multiple sclerosis," I say. "She told me I was going to have a life-changing event."

Greta waves a hand. "I am not impressed. What else did this charlatan say to you?"

"She told me not to marry Nick." I bite down on my thumbnail. "Because... she... she said he was going to kill somebody if I did."

Greta stares at me for a moment. And then she bursts out laughing. "Nick? *Kill* somebody? Oh, you did not believe that, did you? Nick wouldn't hurt a fly! He is just as gentle and kind as my Bernie."

"Well…"

"Listen to me, Rosalie." Her wrinkled face becomes serious again. "Very few people have the gift. But I do. Let me tell your fortune."

I say yes. Just to shut her up.

She turns down the lights first, and as the room descends into darkness, she sits down again on the bed beside me and takes my hands in her cold, wrinkled ones. She closes her eyes, and I can feel the gentle pressure on my fingers.

"You don't use Tarot cards?" I ask.

She scoffs. "Only for charlatans. I do not need them."

I sit there, in my wheelchair, feeling her icy hands in mine. The pressure intensifies and her eyelids flutter. If Nick were here, he would laugh at this display. He doesn't believe in any of this stuff. Neither do I. Not really.

Except I wonder what she's seeing.

"Your future is bright, Rosalie," she says.

I stare at her. "What?"

"I see happiness," she says. "I see great joy coming into your life. Joy like you have never felt before. For you and for Nick."

"Really?" I say flatly.

"I see a happy future for you and Nick. Together. It is your destiny."

I was more willing to believe Nick could be a

murderer. There's no happy future for me and Nick. Everything is different between the two of us now. I fell in love with Nick because I felt like I could tell him anything. But now it's like we're strangers, even though he's constantly helping me with the most intimate things. He doesn't look at me the way he did before. And who could blame him?

No, Nick and I will not have a happy ending.

"Right," I say. "Sure."

She squeezes my hand in hers. For an old woman, she's strong. "I lost my Bernie—it was the greatest tragedy of my life. Do not let Nick get away from you. Do not lose what you have with him. You must protect your marriage at all costs."

I shake my head. "I…"

"Promise me, Rosalie. Promise me you will not let him go. Protect your marriage *at all costs.*"

Her grip on my hand is so tight, it hurts. I try to pull away, but she's too strong. Or I'm too weak. "I… I promise."

She gives me a hard look, then she releases my hand. The imprints of her fingers remain on my skin, darkening into what will become bruises. Greta made me swear not to let him go, but I don't know what she means. If Nick wants to leave, there's nothing I could do to stop him.

CHAPTER 29

Two Years Earlier

Nick is whistling in the shower.

I'll take it as a good sign. He only whistles in the shower when he's in a good mood. Like when I was pregnant. Or every day of our honeymoon. He always whistled in the shower after we had sex.

Well, *that's* definitely not why he's whistling. Before I got sick, we made love every single day, sometimes multiple times. We couldn't get enough of each other. But in the years after my diagnosis, it's become less frequent. Once a week. Then once a month. Lately, every time he reaches for me, I cringe and push him away. He's stopped trying. It's been…

I'm not even sure how long it's been. A very long time.

Nick comes out of the bathroom with the towel wrapped around his waist. He smiles at me. "Good morning, Rosie."

"Morning," I mumble.

He's so sexy in just that towel. The years have been good to him. The problem is me. The thought of being with *anyone*—even my sweet, sexy husband—makes me sick.

I watch as he throws on some clothing. He is still whistling to himself. I squirm under the blanket, feeling sweaty and greasy.

"Ready to get up?" he asks.

I nod.

As he helps me transfer from a bed into my wheelchair, I catch a whiff of aftershave. Nick rarely wears aftershave. Why is he suddenly so concerned with smelling good?

At first, I was pleased about the whistling. But now I feel distinctly uneasy. Why is my husband so happy all of a sudden? Why is he in such a good mood? And why does he take an extra second to check out his appearance in the bathroom mirror before he leaves for the motel?

Fortunately, I have an excellent view of the motel from my bedroom window.

It doesn't take long to have the answer to my question. Later in the morning, I see Nick outside the motel, talking to a curvy blonde who is several years younger than me. I've seen her before out the window, maybe yesterday or the day before. The point is, she's been staying at the motel for several days. And now she's talking to my husband.

I wrench the window open, trying to hear their conversation. But they're too far away, and I only catch a few snippets. I hear him call her Christina. She calls him Nicky, and then she reaches out and adjusts the crooked collar of his shirt. He grins at her.

I know that look.

Then they go into the motel together. My heart is pounding as they disappear from my sight. Despite what I saw, it's hard for me to believe Nick is cheating on me. He's not like that. He's a good person. He wouldn't cheat. He *wouldn't*.

I fumble for my phone and pick his number out from the favorites. After a couple of rings, he picks up. "Rosie? Is everything okay?"

I never call him. It's not surprising he thinks something terrible has happened. "Yes, I just…" I wrack my brain, trying to think of a plausible reason for having called him randomly. "I was wondering if, um, you were going to come back for lunch today."

"I don't know, Rosie." He sounds distracted. "But don't worry. I put that sandwich on the dresser for you. Do you see it?"

I look across the room and see the turkey sandwich he made for me. He even sliced it in half. "Yes. Thank you. I just thought…"

There are voices in the background. Nick is talking to somebody else, but his voice is muffled like he's got his hand over the phone. When he comes back, he still sounds distracted. "Listen, Rosie. I've got to go. I'll see you later."

Before I can say another word, he's hung up on me.

———

"Rosalie, you are a million miles away."

I blink my eyes, focusing on Greta, who is sitting on our bed, a plate on her lap. She brought me a plate of food as well. Greta is a spectacular cook, maybe even better than I am. And certainly better than Nick, whose repertoire includes mostly sandwiches and pasta and overcooked eggs. But no matter what they bring to me, I can't eat more than about a quarter of it—if that. I have no appetite anymore.

"Sorry." I push the goulash around my plate. I've eaten about three bites. "I… I guess I'm not very hungry today."

"Is something wrong?"

"No." I take a gulp from my water glass, thinking of Nick and that gorgeous blonde. "But, um, is there a guest staying at the motel now?"

Greta nods. "Yes. I believe so. She came a few days ago."

I want to blurt out the question that's been running through my head. *Do you think Nick is cheating on me with this woman?* But I can't get myself to say the words.

"Has Nick been in her room much?" I finally ask.

Greta seems surprised by my question. She adores Nick and believes the best of him. She is convinced he is my Prince Charming, and that he and I will live happily ever after. She thinks every man is like her Bernie.

"Not really," she finally says.

"Oh."

Her answer doesn't make me feel much better though. What does she know, anyway? If only I could see better into the room. Then I could reassure myself that nothing is happening.

"Greta," I say. "Do you have a pair of binoculars?"

She blinks at me. "Binoculars?"

"Like, in your room?"

She tilts her head. "I believe so. I have a pair in my trunk. They're old, but binoculars do not expire."

"Do you think I could borrow them?"

"Borrow them?"

"Yes, I…" I force a smile onto my lips, which feel very stiff, like rubber. "I thought I might do some birdwatching. It would help pass the time."

Greta may be a romantic and she may be old, but she's not stupid. She looks beyond my shoulder, out the window. Her face falls. "Oh, Rosalie…"

"Please, Greta." I drop my nearly full plate on top of the dresser. "I know what you're thinking, but it's not like that. It would make me feel better about everything."

"You must trust your husband, Rosalie."

"But—"

"Trust Nick. He is a good man."

"Look, I just…" I take a breath. "I'm stuck here all day, staring out the window. I'd feel better if I could see what was going on in the hotel. You know?"

"It's a mistake."

I squeeze my right hand into a fist. "I don't care."

We are both quiet for a moment. Greta pushes her goulash around with her fork. Seems like she's lost her appetite too. Between me, Nick, and Greta, all three of us have lost weight in the last couple of years. I seem to have that effect on people.

"Can I have them or not?" I finally say.

Greta lets out a long sigh. "I will look in my trunk. See if I can find them."

Later in the afternoon, Greta brings me a dusty old pair of binoculars. I stash them at the bottom of a drawer, where Nick is unlikely to come across them. I feel a rush of relief when I get them in my hands. I didn't think Greta would really come through for me.

But it turns out she was absolutely right.

The binoculars are a huge mistake.

CHAPTER 30

The sun is down and Nick still hasn't gotten back yet.

My back is aching from being in the chair all day. Sometimes I wish I hadn't been so stubborn about not doing physical therapy. I want to get back into bed on my own, but every time I try it, I feel like I'm about to fall. So I always let Nick help me.

I was watching television most of the afternoon, but then I got sick of it and moved to the window. Now I'm watching the moon. It's a full moon tonight—a perfect circle, marred only by the dark smudges that almost look like a man's face. There's something soothing about looking up at that bright white spot in the sky.

And then some movement in one of the windows at the motel catches my eye.

It's that woman's room. Christina.

Even though I shouldn't do it, I take out the pair of binoculars from the dresser drawer where I stashed them. I peer through the lenses and I finally get a good look at this girl, Christina.

She's beautiful. When I was at my best, I could've given her a run for her money. But not now. Not even close. She has long blond hair that shines in the moonlight and breasts that strain at the fabric of her T-shirt. I feel a jolt of jealousy, but I try to push it away. I trust Nick. He loves me.

I can't seem to tear my eyes away from the window. I watch as Christina picks up a brush and runs it through her luxurious blond hair. My hand instinctively goes to my own hair, which has become brittle in the last few years. She smiles at her own reflection—she likes what she sees.

Watching that woman doll herself up makes me miss being pretty. Maybe Nick is right. Maybe I would feel better if I got out of bed more often. Ran a comb through my hair. Put on a dress… Or at least something besides sweatpants or a nightgown.

Something gets Christina's attention. She looks up and walks over to the door. She cracks it open and…

It's Nick.

What is my husband doing in this woman's room?

I watch them through the binoculars, my heart pounding. They're just talking. There's nothing wrong with talking, is there? I mean, yes, they're standing very close to each other. And now she's got her hand on his shoulder.

But that's okay. They're just talking, for God's sake. Nick isn't a cheater. He's a good guy.

I watch his expression through the lenses. He's smiling at her. He looks happy in a way I haven't seen him look in a long time.

And then he leans forward and kisses her.

My heart sinks into my stomach as I watch my husband kiss another woman. And he's not just kissing her. They're *making out*. This isn't the first time, either. You can just tell.

I drop the binoculars on my lap like they're burning.

I take a deep breath, my hands trembling. That bastard. That absolute *bastard*. He's going to be sorry for this.

I fumble for the binoculars again. I look through Christina's window, but they're gone. At least, they're out of my line of sight. Which means they're probably on the bed.

I'm going to kill him.

It's an hour later when I hear his keys in the lock for the front door. An *hour*. Whistling again as his footsteps grow louder up the stairs. A vein pulses in my temple.

"Hey, Rosie," he says as he comes into our bedroom. "What's up?"

I want to punch him in the face. *What's up?* He knows very well what's up. He knows all I've done is sit here all day, so why would he ask me that? He's the one who was across the way, *having sex with another woman.*

"Get out," I say.

He freezes. "What?"

"You heard me." I look him dead in the eyes. "We're done. I want you out."

"Rosie…" His eyes dart around the room. "What's wrong? Why are you so upset?"

"Are you serious?" I spit at him. "Are you really going to pretend like you're not fucking a guest at the motel?"

His mouth falls open and all the color drains out of his face. "You…"

"I saw you through the window, you asshole." I fold my arms across my chest. "Get out. I never want to see you again. Go spend the night with your *girlfriend.*"

To his credit, he doesn't deny it. "I didn't have sex with her. I just kissed her. That's it."

"Oh, that's *it*?"

"Look," he says, "you and I haven't… I mean, not in a *year*…"

"You're absolutely right. Our marriage is over. And now you're free. Congratulations."

"Rosie…"

"I said, get *out*, Nick."

I don't know what I expected Nick to do, but what I don't expect is the way his eyes fill with tears. I've never seen him cry before. He even kept it together in front of me when we lost the baby, although I caught him with bloodshot eyes a couple of times. But now I'm scared he might lose it.

"Rosie." He sits beside me on the bed and runs a shaking hand through his hair. "Please don't do this. I *love* you. I made a huge mistake. Don't do this."

"I'm sorry. My mind is made up."

"But…" He looks down at my legs on the footrests of my chair. "What will you do?"

"I'll figure it out. It's not your problem anymore."

I have a very specific plan for what I'm going to do after Nick leaves. I have a lot of medications in the medicine cabinet in the bathroom. I can just barely stand well enough to reach them. My plan is to take all of them.

It will be a relief to be done.

"Please don't do this." Nick reaches for my hand, and I don't shake him away. "Rosie, I love you. I'm so sorry. *Please*. Give me another chance."

I look into his brown eyes. All I see is love. He doesn't seem like he's sticking around because he feels sorry for me or out of obligation. He wants to be with me. Even after everything I've put him through, he still wants to be with me.

But I keep seeing his arms around that other woman. The way he kissed her… he certainly wasn't thinking of me then.

"I'm sorry," I say. "I can't forgive you."

"Please, Rosie." He squeezes my hand. "You have to give me one more chance. Please let me make this right. I can make this right. I swear."

"Nick…"

"I love you." A single tear gathers in the corner of his right eye, but he swipes at it before it falls. "I promise you, I'm going to fix this."

"Get out."

He takes a deep breath. "Okay. I'll go. For *now*."

Whatever. I'll be dead soon anyway.

He glances at our bed, where we've been sleeping side-by-side for the last year without even touching each other. "Do you need help getting into…?"

"No. I'll manage."

He looks doubtful, but he stands up—something I can't do anymore without support. He takes one last look at me, then he leaves the room, shutting the door gently behind him.

I wonder if this is what that psychic foretold at the carnival all those years ago. He's effectively killed me, even if he doesn't know it.

I consider enacting my plan right then and there. I'm so sick of everything—it will be nice to just be done. Then again, Nick might come back and save me. And if he discovers what I was trying to do, he'll have me put in a psych ward. As if someone in my situation would have to be crazy to want to kill themselves.

Ultimately, I'm just too tired to go through with it. I'm literally *too tired* to kill myself.

Instead, I attempt to transfer myself to the bed. I've done it a handful of times, but usually with Nick nearby. Dr. Heller tried to convince me this is something I should be able to do myself, but I couldn't motivate myself to go to physical therapy and learn. Now I'm paying the price. I put one arm on the bed, supporting myself. I hold on to the armrest of my wheelchair, preparing to scoot myself over.

It should be no surprise that I fall. But somehow, it still is.

I spill out onto the floor in front of my chair. The impact sends a sharp pain through my right hip, and my wheelchair overturns. And moreover, the wind is knocked out of me. For a moment, I just sit there, stunned.

And then I have to figure out what to do. I'm lying on the floor of my bedroom, incapable of getting back into my chair or onto the bed. I don't have any idea what to do next. Crawl over to my phone? Call 911?

I wish I hadn't been so lazy and just taken those pills like I planned.

I drop my head down against the floor and sob. I hate what my life has become. I used to have everything. A loving, faithful, *sexy* husband. The job of my dreams. A baby on the way. And then in three short years, I lost it all.

I wish the floor would just swallow me up.

I've been sobbing for several seconds when I hear the soft knock on the door. At first, I think I must be hearing things. Then the voice: "Rosie?"

It's Nick.

I want to tell him to go away, but even more, I want to get off the floor. "Yes. Come in."

He opens the door and catches me lying there with my red eyes and wet face. "Rosie," he murmurs.

The tears stream down my face. "Nick…"

He bends down beside me, and very, very gently, he lifts me off the floor. He lowers me down on the bed, then he crawls into the bed beside me. He brushes a wet strand of hair from my face as he looks into my eyes. And then, very slowly and gently, he dips his lips onto mine.

We make love for the first time in almost a year. I fall asleep curled up in Nick's arms.

CHAPTER 31

I wake up in the middle of the night and Nick's side of the bed is empty.

I rub my eyes until the clock by our bed comes into focus. It's after three in the morning. I listen for the sound of running water coming from the bathroom but I hear nothing. The house is silent.

"Nick?" I call out.

No answer.

My stomach churns. I thought Nick and I reconnected last night, but maybe I was wrong. Maybe it was a disappointment to him and made him realize he wanted that other woman more. Maybe that's where he is right now. With *her*.

Before I can stop myself, I fumble around in the drawer next to my bed, feeling around for the binoculars.

My fingers close around the cool metal and I pull them out. I'm close enough to the window that I have a good view of the motel. Of Christina's room.

I focus the binoculars on the room where I saw Nick kissing that woman earlier tonight. But even with the lenses, I can't see a thing. The room is dark.

Damn.

I sit up in bed, propping myself up against the pillows, trying to get a better look. And that's when I see some movement along the back of the motel. Near the dumpster.

It's Nick.

What's he doing over there?

I focus in the best I can on his face. He's not smiling. He dumps a black trash bag in the dumpster, then he wipes sweat from his brow with the back of his hand. He takes a step back, staring at the dumpster. He wipes his hands on his jeans, then starts back to our house.

What the hell was he doing there at three in the morning?

When Nick disappears from my view, I yank the drawer open and throw the binoculars inside before he can see them. My heart is pounding as his footsteps grow louder on the stairs outside the door. A few moments later, Nick's silhouette appears in the doorway.

The first thing he does is go to the bathroom. He washes his hands for at least two minutes. There's a rule that you're supposed to sing the happy birthday song to know how long to wash, but he washes far longer than that. He finally comes out of the bathroom, strips off his jeans and T-shirt, and quietly slips onto the mattress beside me, trying hard not to wake me.

Too bad I'm already wide awake.

"Nick?" I whisper.

I hear him inhale sharply beside me. "Oh. I didn't realize you were awake."

I wait for him to explain where he just was. When he says nothing, I say, "Where did you go?"

"I just…" He shifts on the mattress next to me. "I needed some fresh air."

He lied to me. He wasn't just getting some fresh air. He was doing something by the motel. But why would he lie?

Nick reaches over and wraps his arm around me. He tugs my body close to his. "I'm sorry I woke you up. Go back to sleep."

I close my eyes but it takes a long time to go back to sleep.

———

When Nick helps me into my wheelchair the next morning, I hear a noise coming from outside the window. I almost reach for my binoculars, but I can't do that with Nick here. Anyway, I don't need my binoculars to see what the noise is. There's a garbage truck right outside the window.

I keep my eyes pinned on the garbage truck. It goes

around the side of the motel. I watch as the contents of the garbage bin are emptied into the truck. In another couple of hours, everything in the bin will be at the local dump.

"I forgot today is garbage day," I say.

Nick raises his eyebrows at me. "Yeah, it's always Monday. I guess it's been a while since you… Anyway, yes. The garbage truck is always here bright and early Monday morning."

And whatever he put in that dumpster at three in the morning is now gone. He made sure of that.

Instead of the usual peck on the forehead before he leaves, Nick leans in to give me a luxurious kiss on the lips. Despite everything, I feel a stirring of attraction for him. Maybe I'm not entirely dead inside. Ironically, maybe him kissing another woman was what we needed to give our marriage a shot in the arm.

But I'm still going to keep an eye on Christina's room today.

"Maybe tonight we could have a nice dinner together?" he suggests.

I grin at him. "You're a terrible cook though."

"Hey!" He clutches his chest, mock offended. "Well, I could ask Greta to make us something. I know you love her cooking." He pauses. "Or we could go out somewhere."

The idea of venturing out into the real world makes me feel like a hand is squeezing my chest. The only places I go anymore are to doctors' appointments. "Let's ask Greta."

To his credit, Nick doesn't push me. "Okay."

He kisses me one more time, then he goes off to the motel. I watch him walk across the pathway from our house to the front of the building. I wait until he's inside before I reach for my binoculars.

I focus on Christina's room. I recognize there's a chance he might go up there to tell her it's over between the two of them. He knows I can see the room from here, even though he doesn't know about the binoculars. So I'm sure he'll be careful.

But when I zero in on the room, it's still dark.

I look down at my watch. Nick usually doesn't head over there until later in the morning, and it's nearly ten o'clock now. Surely she would be up by now, right? Unless she checked out. Or went out somewhere.

But no. Her Nissan is still in the parking lot. There's nowhere she could have gone on foot.

Christina is still in the motel.

So why is her room dark?

———

It's just after seven when I see Nick leaving the motel with a large Tupperware container of Greta's stew.

I've kept my eyes on Christina's room the entire day. I haven't seen the lights go on once. There's been no movement inside the room. As far as I can see, there's no one in that room.

Yet her car is still in the parking lot.

I hide my binoculars once again when I hear the front door slam shut, followed by Nick's steps on the stairs. I feel a tinge of fear in the pit of my stomach. I felt so many things for my husband in the time we've been together, but this sensation of fear is new.

The door to the bedroom sticks a bit, and it takes a few seconds from him to get it open. He bursts into our bedroom, a grin splitting his face. He proudly holds up the Tupperware container with two plates on top.

"Dinner!" he announces.

I attempt to return his smile. "Oh. Great."

"Do you want it up here?" He sets down the Tupperware on a dresser. "Or we could go down and eat in the dining room. We haven't done that in a long time. I could carry you and—"

"Did you ask Christina to leave?" I interrupt him. It's all I can think about.

"I'm sorry." Splatters of red appear on his neck. "No, I didn't. I tried to tell her but every time I knocked on her door, she didn't answer."

"I see…" I tug at the sleeve of my shirt. "And she's definitely still in the motel?"

"Well, yeah. I mean, her car is still there."

"Yeah…"

He runs a hand through his hair. "I wasn't with her at all today. I swear to you. I'll only see her one more time to tell her to leave. That's it."

I want to believe him. But where is she?

And what was he doing at three in the morning?

He sits on the bed, close to me. He reaches for my hand, and I allow him to squeeze it in his own. "You believe me, right, Rosie?"

What can I say to him but yes?

CHAPTER 32

The next morning, I'm in my eternal perch by the window when the police cars arrive in the motel parking lot. Not just one police car. Police *cars*. Plural. And not just that, but there's also an ambulance.

Fear grips my stomach. Is it Greta? She's so old. Maybe she fell and broke her hip.

But why would the police cars be there?

I retrieve my binoculars from the dresser drawer and look out at the parking lot, although I don't need them. The police officers are getting out of their vehicle and heading straight to the entrance to the motel. They're not here to book a room, that's for sure.

I grab my phone and call Nick. Naturally, it goes right to voicemail. So does my second call. After several more tries, he finally picks up.

"I can't talk, Rosie." His voice is low and serious. "The police are here."

"Why? What's going on?"

The silence on the other line seems to last for an eternity before he answers. "Christina is dead."

"Dead? What are you talking about?"

There are muffled voices in the background. "I've got to go. I'll talk to you later."

And then he hangs up on me.

I try calling him again. And again. But he must've turned off his phone, because all the calls go right to voicemail. I get out my binoculars again and look out at Christina's room. The police officers are in there now, and so is Nick. They're talking. It doesn't look like they're handcuffing him or anything like that—that's a good sign.

But what happened to Christina? If she's dead, what are the chances that it was from natural causes? She was only in her twenties. People don't just drop dead randomly at that age.

I watch all morning, intermittently browsing my phone to see if there are any news stories about her, except I don't even know her last name. They bring out the stretcher, with a sheet covering the body underneath.

So it's true. Christina is dead.

The woman my husband was kissing two nights ago is dead.

Now there's a police officer talking to Nick outside the motel. I shove my binoculars back in the drawer and wrench the window open, but I can't hear what they're saying. But then Nick points to our house. The officer nods, and now they're both walking toward our front door.

I run my fingers through my hair, trying to prepare myself to see this stranger. I'm wearing a T-shirt and sweatpants, which is what I wear most days. At least my clothes are clean. And I had a shower yesterday morning, although my hair still feels limp and greasy.

After a minute, there's a knock on the bedroom door. "Yes?" My voice cracks. "Come in."

The door swings open and there they are. My husband and the police officer. The officer is about Nick's height, with dark hair and imposing dark eyes. He's absolutely terrifying.

"This is my wife, Rosalie," Nick says.

The officer's eyes rake over me. He glances back at Nick. "*That's* your wife?"

Nick glares at him. "Right. That's what I just said."

I can't blame the officer for being skeptical. There was a time when I used to be beautiful, but I'm not anymore. Not by any stretch of the imagination. I avoid looking in the mirror these days, because when I do, a stranger stares back at me. I always have dark circles under my eyes and hollow cheeks that made me look ten years older than I am. My formally thick dark brown hair has lost all its luster. Nick is a good-looking guy, and the officer probably wonders what he's doing stuck with me.

It's probably a little suspicious as well.

"Mrs. Baxter," the officer says, "I'm Detective Esposito. I don't know how much you heard about what happened out there…"

I bite my lip. "Nick said one of our guests was… dead?"

"It looks like she was murdered, actually," Esposito says. My stomach sinks—my fears are true. "She was stabbed in the chest."

I look over at Nick, who is staring down at his sneakers, his face pale.

"I'm wondering if I could ask you a few questions, Mrs. Baxter," Esposito says.

"Of course," I manage.

When Nick doesn't budge, the detective shoots him a look. "Mr. Baxter, would you step outside so I could talk to your wife?"

Nick looks like he's going to be sick. He nods. "Sure. Rosie, if you need anything…"

"She'll be fine," Esposito snaps at him. "We're just going to have a talk."

My brain is going a mile a minute as my husband leaves the room and shuts the door behind him, leaving me alone with the terrifying detective. I lift my eyes to look at him.

"How are you doing, Mrs. Baxter?" he asks.

"Fine," I squeak.

"I just have a few questions for you about the motel. Your husband mostly runs it?"

I nod. "Yes. I haven't been able to recently. I... I can't get around so easily anymore."

"He told me you have multiple sclerosis and you can't walk at all. Is that accurate?"

I flinch at the way he phrased it so harshly. "Yes."

"When is the last time you've been inside the motel?"

"It's been... a while."

"Days? Weeks? Months?"

"At least a year," I admit.

He looks over my shoulder, out the window. "You got a pretty good view of the motel from here?"

"Yes. I suppose."

"Did you see anything suspicious in the last two days?" He taps his fingers against the top of my dresser. "Any suspicious strangers coming in or out of the hotel?"

"No."

"Anything suspicious at all?"

I close my eyes for an instant, and I can see my husband disposing of something in the dumpster in the middle of the night. I open my eyes again and stare at the detective. "Nothing I can remember."

He cocks his head to the side. "Did you ever meet Christina Marsh?"

Christina Marsh. That's her name. I shake my head no.

"Do you know if your husband was friendly with her?"

My heart is beating so fast, it's making me dizzy. "I... I don't know. I don't think so."

Detective Esposito's black eyebrows draw together. "What's your relationship with your husband?"

"My relationship with my husband? What do you mean? He's my husband."

"How long have you been married?"

"Seven years."

"And he... takes care of you?"

I narrow my eyes. "Yes. I mean, sort of."

"He told me he helps you get dressed, shower, get in and out of bed. He makes your meals too. Is that right?"

I imagine the conversation Nick must've had with the detective, and I feel sick. "Yes... sort of..."

"So really, he's more of your caregiver than anything..."

My eyes snap up. "What are you saying?"

"Mrs. Baxter, I'm just trying to get an accurate picture of your marriage."

I hate what he was implying. Even worse, I hate that he's right. Even though Nick and I reconnected for a night, things still aren't the same as they used to be. It's not anything like before. It never will be.

"Mrs. Baxter," he says, "I have to ask you this, and I hope you'll tell me the truth."

My heart sinks. "Okay..."

"Was your husband having an affair with Christina Marsh?"

"No," I say, but the lie catches in my throat.

"Are you absolutely certain?"

"Yes."

I try to adjust myself in my wheelchair, but it sets off a spasm in my right leg. I grab it with my hands, trying to calm my jumping limb. Because of the lesions in my spinal cord, my legs sometimes do what they want to do and I can't control it. It takes me almost a minute of readjusting my leg until it stops jumping. When I look up again, I see pity in the detective's eyes.

"Are you all right, Mrs. Baxter?"

I swallow. "Yes. I'm fine. I think I've answered all your questions."

He hesitates, then finally nods. "I'm going to go downstairs and talk to your husband again."

After Detective Esposito leaves the bedroom, I watch him again through the window, talking to Nick. Even from here, Nick is visibly upset. At any moment, I expect the detective to snap a pair of handcuffs on my husband. But he doesn't.

The police cars linger for a long while, but eventually, they all take off. It isn't until nearly one o'clock that Nick raps on the door to our bedroom with a plate of food in his hand. My lunch. He brings it to me every day.

"How are you doing?" he asks me.

"Been better. How are *you* doing?"

"Been better." He sinks down onto the bed and puts the plate down next to him. "Rosie, you don't think that

I…?"

I wasn't going to say anything. I planned to keep my silence till the day we died, but I can't do it. I have to tell him. "I saw you."

"You…"

"I saw you at the dumpster," I say. "In the middle of the night two nights ago. At three in the morning. What were you doing there?"

The panic spreads across his handsome features. "I was taking out the garbage."

"At three in the morning? Do you think I'm stupid?"

"I *was*." His hands are shaking as he tugs at his T-shirt hem. "Look, I got distracted by, you know, what happened with Christina, and I forgot to take it out to the dumpster. The truck arrives early in the morning, and I was worried if I didn't put it out then, I'd miss it."

He's looking me right in the eye when he says it. Is it possible he's telling the truth? That he was up at three in the morning simply *taking out the trash*? "But how come you told me you were getting some air? You *lied*."

"I know." He squeezes his knees. "I lied to you. But I didn't want to remind you about what I had done—why I'd been too distracted to take out the trash—and it just seemed easier."

I don't know what to say to that. Do I believe him? I'm not sure.

He shakes his head. "What do you think I was

throwing out?"

"I don't know. Bloody clothing that you were wearing."

I hear the sharp inhale of his breath. "Rosie…"

"You asked me."

"I *didn't* kill her." His voice sounds choked. "I swear to you. I'd never do anything like that. The police think I did it, but…" He buries his face in his hands. "Christ, this sucks."

"Nick…"

He raises his face to look at me. "Please tell me you believe me. Tell me you don't think I killed her."

That night I confronted him about her, Nick promised he would make things right. He swore it. That night, Nick was skulking around the hotel at three in the morning. And the next morning, the other woman was dead. Stabbed to death. And Nick is the only person who had the key to her room.

"I believe you," I lie.

That psychic at the carnival was right. My husband is a murderer. And it's all because of me.

CHAPTER 33

One Day Earlier

Even through the snow and darkness, I can see how attractive she is.

She has blond hair, the same as Christina Marsh did. She's clutching her luggage as she shuffles through the freezing rain from her car to the motel door. I watch from my perch at the bedroom window, willing her to turn around. But she doesn't turn around. She pushes the door open and goes inside.

She probably doesn't know the motel's sordid history. We have quite the reputation. The Murder Motel, they called us.

It's been two years since Christina Marsh was found

murdered in room 201. For a couple of weeks, I was certain Nick was going to be taken away in handcuffs, but ultimately, they never arrested him. It's a good thing, because we were broke enough as it was, and we never could have afforded a decent lawyer. But the consensus on the Internet was that he murdered her.

Even my family thought he was a killer. My mother called me up a week after it all went down. "Come home, Rosalie. You can't stay with that man."

She always called me Rosalie. Everyone called me Rosalie. Nick is the only one who ever called me Rosie.

"I'm not leaving my husband," I told her.

"He cheated on you and then killed that girl. Watch— you'll be next."

"Mom!"

But I wasn't surprised. My mother was never supportive of anything I did, including marrying Nick. It didn't matter that I loved him. She thought I could do better. Not that I could do better these days. If I weren't with Nick, I would be alone for the rest of my life.

Nick has been doing what he can to make money. He took some online web design courses, and now he is doing freelance work so we don't go broke. He's been talking about trying to sell the motel, but after Christina was killed there, he can't pay somebody to take it off his hands.

He usually does his freelance computer work at the front desk in the motel. Never here. He doesn't want to be around me anymore, and it's hard to blame him. After what happened with Christina, our relationship got even worse, if that were possible. We barely speak two words to each other anymore. We haven't made love once since her death.

Sometimes I'm not sure we ever will again.

I see movement in the motel on the second floor. Then the lights flicker on in room 203. Nick has chosen a room for the guest.

And now I get out my binoculars.

Nick still doesn't know about the binoculars, and that I've been using them to spy on his guests—he'd be furious. I have tried to use restraint about it. I don't spy on him all the time. For the most part, the binoculars stay shut in a drawer. But sometimes I get them out in an emergency.

An attractive woman showing up at the motel counts as an emergency. Hey, it's not my fault that my husband has proven himself not to be trustworthy.

Sometimes when I'm staring across into the hotel with my binoculars, I feel ill about what my life has become. That night two years ago, Nick stopped me before I took all those pills in my medicine cabinet. But the truth is, I still think about it a lot. Except now it's too late. I can't stand on my own anymore, even when holding onto the sink, and the pills are too high for me to reach. So I keep on living, by default.

I raise the binoculars to my eyes and look into room 203. Close up, she is decidedly very pretty. Maybe in her late twenties. Blond hair. A little bony compared with Christina, but still very attractive. I watch as she paces across the room. She looks anxious.

I wonder if she's in any trouble. After all, she pulled into a seedy motel in the middle of the snowstorm.

Or maybe she's here to *make* trouble.

She pauses for a moment. She walks over to the door to her room and flings it open. Nick is standing there, holding a plate of food out to her.

Gosh, isn't he nice? The kind, handsome owner of the motel thoughtfully brought her some dinner. I bet he didn't even charge her, as if we could spare the money. I can just imagine her swooning over that one.

I watch them chatting for a moment, wishing I could hear what they're saying. But more than that, I wish I could trust him.

But I can't.

CHAPTER 34

That Morning

Nick is rifling around in our closet. I turn my chair to watch him, trying to figure out what he's doing. "What are you doing?"

"I need to borrow your boots."

"My boots?"

"I'm going to help this guest dig her car out and she doesn't have any boots. I'll bring them back when she's done with them."

My jaw tightens, as I remember watching that woman's pretty face through my binoculars last night. "Is it really necessary for you to dig her car out?"

"I told her I'd help. Although honestly, I don't think

she's going anywhere until the plow comes."

"Well, gee, that's *so* nice of you." I don't even try to keep the edge out of my voice.

Nick retrieves my fur lined black boots from the closet. I remember how warm those boots used to be. I could go out in deep snow, and I wouldn't even feel it. Of course, I wouldn't feel it now either since I can't feel my feet at all.

"Rosie," he says patiently. "I have to help her. Don't be difficult about this."

"Oh, am I being difficult?"

He frowns. "Yes. You are."

"Strange. Why would I be upset because my husband wants to help a beautiful young woman with her car?"

He drops the boots on the ground and sits down heavily on the bed. "Don't do this. Please."

"Do what?"

"I've been faithful, okay?" He looks me in the eyes. "I haven't touched another woman since… Anyway, it's not like you've done anything to help."

"Help what?" I stare back at him. "I'm stuck here in this room all the time. What am I supposed to do?"

"For starters, get out of this goddamn room. Let me turn the dining room downstairs into a bedroom. Let me convert the kitchen at Rosalie's and we can open it back up—"

"You've *got* to be kidding me." I punch my fist into my knee so hard, it kicks up a spasm. But I just ignore it. "You act like it's all so easy. It's not easy."

"I know it's not easy, but—"

"You *don't* know." My right leg trembles with a muscle spasm. "Look, I don't want to have this conversation. Go give that woman my boots. Let her keep them, for all I care. It's not like I'm ever going to use them again."

I expect him to keep arguing with me, like he often does. But instead, he gets back on his feet. "Fine," he snaps.

Then he picks up the boots and stomps out the door. Every step he takes echoes through the entire house until the front door slams shut.

After he leaves, I wheel myself over to the window. And I grab my binoculars. I shouldn't watch them, but I can't help myself. Worrying about Nick cheating on me again has become an obsession. When we were young, I always trusted him. I was never jealous. Now it's all I can think about.

I peer through my binoculars, searching for that woman's car. She parked it in the lot by Rosalie's. It's a strange thing to do, considering the motel has its own lot. Why would she have parked at Rosalie's, which is boarded up? And she didn't just park at Rosalie's, she parked all the way around back.

What does she have to hide?

A few minutes later, I see the two of them come into view. The woman is wearing a thick coat, but I remember catching that glimpse of her in room 203. She's beautiful.

And Nick knows it.

Mostly, they're digging out her car. Nick is doing most of the work, because he's big and strong and he always wants to help. I watch their lips move through the binoculars. They're talking. At one point, he laughs at something she says.

When is the last time I've seen Nick laugh? I swear, it's got to have been a year, at least.

They would make a good couple. They look better together than Nick and I do these days, that's for sure. I'm sure he feels some sort of tug of attraction towards her. He's got to be tempted.

Before I can stop myself, I reach for my phone. I select his number and wait for it to ring. Through the binoculars, I can tell he feels it buzzing in his pocket. He steps away from the car, pulls out his phone and looks at the number. Will he take my call when he's with his beautiful motel guest?

He does.

"Rosie?" he says. "What's wrong?"

"Having fun digging out that car? Maybe you should have a snowball fight."

There's a long pause on the other line. "I'm just helping her dig out her car, Rosie. She's stuck in the snow."

"I'll bet."

"Come on, Rosie. That's not fair."

"Fair to whom?"

He lets out a long sigh. "What do you want me to do? I have to help. It's the decent thing to do."

"Right. And you always do the decent thing, don't you, Nick?"

He doesn't take the bait, which makes my words seem jealous and petty. "I'll be done here soon. Is there something you need?"

"Tell your little friend to keep my boots. They look good on her."

Nick raises his eyes to look up at our house. I quickly lower the binoculars, even though he can't possibly tell I have them from all the way over there. If he knew I was spying on him with binoculars... Well, I'm not sure what he would do. Probably nothing. But the whole thing is embarrassing.

"I'll be back later," he mumbles.

Then he disconnects the call.

Even though I shouldn't, I keep watching them. They don't quite manage to get her car unstuck, which isn't surprising because we got hit hard by snow. But it means they return to the motel together. At one point, she stumbles in the snow and he catches her.

She's still got my boots on. I wonder if she really will keep them. The thought is like a knife in my chest.

I doze off after that. I always get so tired in the afternoon. Sometimes if Nick is around, I ask him to put me back in bed, but most of the time, I just sleep in my wheelchair. It's easier that way.

When I wake up, Nick is in her room.

I reach into the drawer by the bed and pull out my binoculars so I can get a better look. They're sitting together on the bed. No, not just sitting together. He's rubbing her back. They're talking, but I can't hear what they're saying.

I wonder if I can persuade Greta to put a listening device in room 203.

No. Too far.

My heart is pounding as I watch him. But Nick isn't doing anything wrong. They're just sitting together and talking. There's nothing wrong with talking.

Until they start kissing.

CHAPTER 35

I can't believe what I'm seeing. He *swore* to me he would never do anything like that again. Yet here he is, kissing another woman. Breaking his marriage vows for a second time.

Not that I'm surprised. I mean, that's why I got the binoculars.

It's a little different this time. They're not making out like he was with Christina. He kisses her, then he jumps up off the bed. He's gesturing with his arms. Then he looks out the window.

Shit. He sees me.

I lower the binoculars and throw them onto the bed. Did he see the binoculars? I'm not sure about that. I hope not.

Even without the binoculars, I can see him exit the other woman's room. Probably coming over here to grovel.

Again. I have to put those binoculars away quickly, before he spots them. Then I have to decide if I'll forgive him. I probably will. It gets easier each time, and I have to admit, I don't know what I would do without him. Even more than two years ago, Nick has become my caregiver. That is the crux of our relationship now. We are not husband and wife anymore, only caregiver and patient.

Also, I don't want things to end up like last time. As much as I want to wrap my fingers around this woman's pretty little neck, I don't want to see her stabbed to death. I know what my husband is capable of now. I can't let it happen again.

Unfortunately, when I tossed the binoculars onto the bed, they went all the way across the bed and rolled off the other side. So I can't just grab them and throw them into the drawer. There isn't much time either.

I push back on the wheels of my chair, backing away from the bed. The bedroom isn't all that big, and it's hard to maneuver. I end up having to do the equivalent of a five point turn to get out of the space between the bed and the wall. By the time I've freed myself, I can hear Nick's footsteps on our stairs.

He's in the house. He'll be in the bedroom any second.

I make one last ditch effort to get to the binoculars, but it's too late. He bursts into the room, his face red, his short dark blond hair messy from the wind.

"Rosie," he gasps. "That was... I didn't..."

I fold my arms across my chest. "That wasn't you kissing her?"

"She kissed *me*."

"And I'm sure you did nothing at all to lead her on."

"I didn't! Rosie, you have to believe me…" He trails off as his eyes land on the binoculars on the floor. My heart is thudding as he bends down to pick them up, a baffled expression on his face. "What the fuck is this?"

I don't know what to say.

"Are you *spying* on me?" He shakes the binoculars. "With binoculars? Seriously?"

"Do you blame me? Look at what I caught you doing."

I expect him to protest again, but instead, his shoulders sag and he tosses the binoculars on the bed. "You know what? I can't do this anymore."

"Do what?"

"I love you, Rosie," he says softly. "But you don't trust me anymore. You won't leave the room or have a conversation with me. You don't even let me touch you unless I'm helping you. I tried—I really did. But it's obvious you don't want me here anymore. And I… I'm not sure I want to be here anymore."

I stare up at him. I can see in his brown eyes that he means it. I finally pushed him too far. He's done. "I see."

"We're both miserable," he says. The understatement of the century. "I think it's time to call it quits."

I had thought my life was as awful as it could possibly

be, but at the moment, my heart rips in two. "I agree."

"I mean, do you even still love me anymore?"

I look up at his face. He's still the same guy who tripped over his own feet while running track in high school because he couldn't stop staring at me. The same guy who bought me a restaurant so that I could have my dream. We've been together for eighteen years, and all but the last five were so happy. Maybe we used up all our happiness. Maybe everybody only gets so much.

Do I still love him? Of course I do. He's the only man I ever loved. The only man I ever *will* love. But he has a chance to be happy again. I don't.

"No," I say. "I don't."

He looks like he's about to break down, but to his credit, he keeps it together. He always does. "Fine," he says. "I'll move out."

"Fine." I feel oddly calm about the fact that the love of my life is walking out on me. "You should sell this house. I'll go stay with my parents."

"Fine."

"Fine."

Now that we have each reassured each other that everything is fine four times, he turns and leaves the bedroom. I watch him go. The ache in my chest is so painful, I want to scream. *Please don't go, Nick! I love you! How could you ever think otherwise?*

But that would be wrong. The right thing is to let him

go.

I take out my phone. I type into the search engine: easiest way to commit suicide.

CHAPTER 36

I spend a good hour searching websites, trying to figure out how I'm going to do it.

The search immediately brings up a suicide hotline. But that's for normal people, who are just depressed. My life is *actually* hopeless. I would be better off dead, and I know it.

Even the websites that tell you how to do it are still trying to talk you out of it. *Think of the people who care about you.* Yeah, right. I've got a husband, who is walking out on me. I've got my parents, who I have disappointed every step of the way. Really, the website doesn't get it. If they knew me, they wouldn't bother trying to talk me out of it.

My physical limitations will make this tricky. I can't jump out the window or off a building. Hanging myself is way too labor intensive. I'll have to go the medication route.

Nick will have to give me my pill bottles before I move out. Or I can ask Dr. Heller for a prescription for a sleeping pill.

I haven't quite decided on a plan yet, but I'm tired from thinking about it. I look back up, out the window, and see a woman moving around room 203. But it isn't the blond woman. This woman has dark hair.

Unless it's the same woman, and she just dyed her hair. That's a possibility.

Nick dropped the binoculars onto the bed, within my reach. I grab for them and focus on the window again. I zoom in close to the woman in room 203.

It's somebody different. Somebody older. Curvier. Definitely an unfamiliar face.

I guess the blond woman must've left, and he gave the room to a new guest. I look down at my watch. It's barely been an hour. Quick turnaround.

I watch this new woman for a minute, but she doesn't seem to be doing much. Her head is bent, and she seems to be looking down at her phone.

I drop the binoculars on my lap. My life has become pathetic. I'm watching a woman surf the Internet on her phone.

I wish I could just end it all right now.

Then the woman's eyes lift from her phone. She's looking straight at the window. Right at me.

I push my hand against my wheels, backing up a foot. At least she didn't catch me holding the binoculars. But there's something about this woman that's making me uneasy. Not jealousy—that's become a very familiar emotion lately. Something else unnerving.

My phone buzzes from where I left it on the bed. I swivel my head and see a text from Nick:

I can help you get into bed tonight.

I grit my teeth. I don't want his pity. Granted, it's something he helps me with every night, so I can see why he feels bad about abandoning me. But I'll manage on my own. I've practiced it a few times since that night I went crashing to the floor.

I type in my reply: *Don't worry about it.*

Fine. But I'll bring you dinner. Don't say no.

I want to tell him not to bother, but that would be stupid. I have become horribly dependent on him over the last five years. If I'd let him turn the dining room into a bedroom like he wanted, I wouldn't have this problem. But I've been stubborn.

Well, he'll be rid of me soon anyway.

I look out the window again. The dark-haired woman in room 203 is gone, although she left the light on in her room. I scan the parking lot and see only one car, which must belong to that woman. But then I notice the parking lot around the building that used to be Rosalie's.

The blond woman's car is still there.

Well, that's strange. I assumed when I saw somebody else in her room, she must've checked out. And Nick himself said that she was very eager to leave. Now that the plow has done its job, why hasn't she taken off?

Again, I get that uneasy feeling. But really, it's none of my business. Nothing here is any of my concern anymore. Including Nick. If he wants to make out with all the guests, that's his business.

I wish I could stop missing him.

I reach for my phone and start scanning through the photos. I haven't taken any pictures in the longest time. I go back in time to seven years ago. Nick got the idea to do a theme night at the diner, and that particular night, we were doing eighties night. I had on a headband and legwarmers, and I had crimped my hair. Nick was wearing double denim—denim jeans with a denim jacket—and he slicked back his hair. We snapped pictures of each other, both of us in the middle of laughing at how stupid we looked. Then I snapped a selfie, but Nick ruined it by kissing me in the middle.

We looked so happy. We *were* happy. I can't even remember what it felt like to be so happy.

After I'm gone, Nick will meet someone else. I'm sure he'll be sad about me for a while, but he'll move on. He'll find some other woman to have this kind of happiness with—I'll just be a distant memory by then. And he can start a family with her. He deserves to be happy. He's a good guy. I'm not sure if I believe he killed that woman two years ago. He's not capable of it. We'll probably never know what really happened to her.

I look up from my phone as some movement from outside the window catches my eye. It's coming from all the way across the parking lot, at my old restaurant. There's somebody in front of the blond woman's car.

At first I think it's the blond woman, but she's wearing a different coat. I grab my binoculars again to get a better look.

It's the dark-haired woman staying in room 203. What on earth is she doing?

Then she looks up, straight at our house. Her eyes point directly at me. I drop the binoculars, my heart pounding. She doesn't look away.

What is going on?

She's rifling around in her purse, looking for something. She pulls something out of her purse, but it's much too far away to see without the binoculars. Cautiously, I bring them back up to my eyes just as she pulls the object from her purse.

I can't see what the object is, but it glints in the moonlight. Could that be...

A knife?

Oh my God, does she have a knife? Why would this woman have a knife? And what does she plan to do with it?

And then she moves in the direction of our house.

My heart is pounding painfully. What is she doing? Why is she coming here with a knife? Is she angry that I was watching her?

I throw the binoculars onto the bed, like they're made of fire. She couldn't have seen that I had them. And even if she did, she wouldn't kill me over it, would she? It's not like I saw anything terrible. I just saw her sitting in her room. That's all.

She's definitely moving toward the house. There's no doubt about it. And she's still got that knife gripped in her hand.

Oh god oh god oh god oh god…

And now she's at our front door. I hear her knock, but I stay perfectly still. But then a horrible thought occurs to me.

Nick may not have locked the front door.

We were always lax about locking doors. After all, it's pretty deserted out here and we never had much worth stealing.

And then I hear the footsteps coming from downstairs. Oh my God. She's inside.

I grab my phone. The first thing I do is text Nick: *Please come here now! Somebody is in the house!* Then I dial 911, although it will be far too late by the time they arrive.

"Emergency services," a female voice says.

"Please help me," I croak. "There's an intruder in my house."

"I'm sorry…. I can't…… you're saying."

Great. The storm must have damaged the closest cell

phone tower.

The footsteps are growing louder, and now I hear a loud creak. She's on the stairs. I don't have much time.

"Please." Tears leap into my eyes. "You've got to help me! There's somebody in my house. In the house next to the Baxter Motel on I-93 N."

"Ma'am……. can't……"

And now the phone is dead.

The creaking noise stops. She must've reached the top of the stairs. In two seconds, she'll be in my bedroom. With that knife.

She's going to kill me.

Isn't this what I wanted though? I was just looking up how to kill myself on Google. And now this stranger is going to do the job for me. Why am I calling 911? I should open the door for her. Welcome her.

Except I realize at this moment that I don't want to die.

As my heart pounds rapidly in my chest, it's like a fog has lifted from my brain. The fog that's been coloring every moment of my life for the last five years. My life isn't hopeless, and I don't want to die. I want my restaurant back. I want to get those contractors in and convert the kitchen so I can use it again even if I can't stand or walk. I want to do a course of physical therapy so that I can take care of myself again and I don't have to depend on Nick for every little thing.

And I want *Nick*. I don't want him to leave. I don't

want him to find some other woman and be happy with her. I want him to be happy with *me* again. I want to start a family with him.

But most of all, I want *him*. I want him so badly. I don't want to die before seeing him again.

The door to my bedroom swings open. The dark-haired woman is standing there in her pea green winter coat, a knife glinting in her right hand. I push my hands against the wheels of my chair and hit the wall behind me.

"You…" she hisses at me.

I raise my hands in the air. "I'm sorry. Whatever you think I did, I'm sorry."

"You know what happened to my sister," she snaps at me.

"Your… sister?" Is she the sister of the blond woman?

She raises the knife and takes a step towards me. "Don't play dumb."

I glance down at my phone. Nick hasn't responded to my text. He probably hasn't even seen it. He'll read it just in time to discover my dead body. "I… I don't know what you're talking about…"

"Liar…"

"Please…" A tear escapes my right eye. "I didn't do anything to your sister. I *swear.*"

She takes another step forward. Her eyes are pools of darkness, staring into mine. "I never said you did."

CHAPTER 37

ROB

Three hours earlier

Most of the time, the first thing I do when I get home is take a shower.

Claudia requires it. Not that it's a terrible idea. When you're working on people's toilets, you get your hands dirty. Claudia claims there's grease and grime permanently ground into the creases of my hands but that's not true. I can get them clean if I want. If I scrub for a long time.

Today was the kind of job where you come home and want to shower right away. There was a clog in the pipe that just wouldn't come free. I worked at it forever before I figured out what it was. It was a dead rat.

No, not a dead rat. A *frozen* dead rat.

Half a frozen dead rat.

So when I walk through the front door of my house, yeah, I want to shower. And after that, a nice dinner with Claudia. Although that's one of those things that's gotten more and more rare lately. Everything is a fight these days. I don't even know why. I work hard all day, and all I want to do is go home and relax at the end of the day with a nice cold beer. You think I want to fight with my wife? I don't.

The house is dark when I get inside. I swear Claudia told me she didn't have any clients this afternoon. On account of the snow.

"Claudia?" I call out.

No answer.

I don't know where she could be. Maybe she's looking for Quinn, although I don't know why she thinks she'll be better at it than the police. Unless she knows something she's not telling me, which might be true.

I don't get Claudia's relationship with Quinn. Quinn is fine. She's nice enough. Quiet compared with my wife. Her husband is an asshole, but who cares? Claudia spends so much time with Quinn, but sometimes I wonder if they even like each other.

Claudia is always whining about Quinn. To be fair, she whines about everything. But especially about Quinn. Quinn's fake blond hair. Quinn's giant house. How Quinn wouldn't give us any money to help when our roof collapsed last year and wrecked our attic.

Not that we need money from the Alexanders. I do fine as a plumber. It's a very good living. Maybe I'm not rich like Derek Alexander, but I could afford to fix my own damn roof. I didn't want their charity. I wouldn't have taken the money if they offered it.

I head up the stairs, trying not to think about where Claudia might be. I don't even know if I care. There was a time when I might have come home and told her about the rat in the pipe and she would have laughed. But these days, she wouldn't want to hear it.

I strip off my dirty clothing and go straight in the shower. I turn it up as hot as it gets, so hot I might get second-degree burns, but it will be worth it. It's *cold* outside. And I installed a shower nozzle to improve the pressure. It was Claudia's request, but I think I like it more than she does.

The water runs over my hair, which admittedly, isn't much to speak of lately. Claudia likes to point out I'm losing my hair, and that it makes me look like an old man. It's a favorite topic of hers. I told her I'll just shave it all off, but she doesn't want that either. I don't know what the hell she wants.

My head is throbbing dully from the stress of getting that goddamn rat out of the pipe. I reach for my forehead and my fingers graze the scar on my hairline. I got that scar a year ago, and it still throbs sometimes. Claudia and I were in a fight—yelling and screaming, and yes, throwing things. I can't even remember what the fight was about, but she picked up a paperweight and threw it at my head. Five stitches.

She felt bad about it though. Drove me to the ER. Was real nice for a good few weeks after. No fighting.

When I climb out of the shower, I wrap a towel around my waist and stare at my reflection in the mirror. I look tired. Yeah, I'm losing my hair, but I don't look that different from the day Claudia and I met. But somehow, she's gotten sick of looking at me.

I tap the medicine cabinet open. We got a lot of pill bottles in there. I don't know what the hell half of them are—they all belong to Claudia. I rifle through half full bottles and finally find the Tylenol. I shake two of them into my hand and swallow them dry. Maybe that will help with the headache.

When I get out of the bathroom, it's strangely quiet. "Claudia?" I call out.

No answer.

Claudia still isn't home. Where the hell is she? It's getting late. Usually we have dinner around now.

I throw on some clothes, and while I'm buttoning my jeans, I hear a ding from the hallway. It's the dryer. Before Claudia left for wherever she was going, she must've put a load of clothes in the dryer.

That's another problem Claudia's got with me. I never

do the wash. Whenever I bring up having a baby, she always says that. *How are you going to help me take care of a baby if you won't even do the laundry?* I don't know what one thing has to do with the other. Everyone else I know who got married when we did has a kid or two by now. What are we waiting for?

But if I need to do the laundry to prove myself to her, hell, I'll do it. I don't mind. It's easier than getting a dead rat out of a pipe.

I go out to the hallway where our washer and dryer are set up. I take the load out of the dryer—it's mostly Claudia's stuff. Shirts and scrubs. I almost think maybe I shouldn't do it because I'll fold her shirts wrong, and that will be another thing I did wrong today. You can't win. But then I say to hell with it. Better to try.

I fold Claudia's shirts the best I can. I build a little stack of them on our bed, and I'm almost proud of it. I recognize a lot of the shirts. She still has that shirt with the silhouette of the Eiffel tower on it. She wore that the day we met. I remember because I liked how she had the French name *and* the French shirt.

I just liked *her* though. Mostly that.

I do a good job with the folding. I mean, it's a nice little pile of shirts. I think I folded them right. She'll be happy. She's got to be happy with this, for once.

Claudia keeps her shirts in the big dresser in our bedroom. I open up the drawer and push some of the clothing aside to make room for the neatly folded clean shirts. And that's when something falls out of the pile of shirts that was already in the drawer.

It's a phone.

I pick it up and turn it over in my hand. It's a burner phone. One of those phones you get when you don't want somebody to track you.

What the hell is my wife doing with a burner phone?

I flip it open. I notice a bunch of missed calls on the screen. I think about calling the number back, but I don't. I want to know what the deal is with this phone first, before I start calling a number and acting like an idiot.

There are a bunch of text messages on the phone. All from the same number. I open up the most recent one:

I can't wait to see you.

What the...?

I sink onto the bed as I read through the text messages one by one. It gets much worse.

She just went out. See you soon!

Rob won't be home till late. Come over.

I can't wait to get you naked.

You're all I can think about.

Well, great. Claudia is messing around with another guy.

Am I surprised? I don't even know. Am I pissed off? Hell *yes*. How could she? How could she do something like that to me? To *us*? I knew she wasn't happy with me, but what the hell? We could've talked it out. Marriage counseling or some shit like that.

I squeeze the phone, feeling it almost crack in my hand. I want to throw it across the room and watch it shatter. I know I shouldn't. This is the only evidence I have that she's been messing around on me. But the urge is almost too strong.

And then the phone rings.

CHAPTER 38

It's the same number that's been texting her and calling her. The guy. He's trying to reach her. She's probably forgotten about some get-together they had because she's been too focused on Quinn.

Some of my anger fades. Claudia is going through a lot right now with Derek being killed and Quinn maybe being held hostage. Not that it's any excuse for what she did. But she's already distraught.

That doesn't mean I'm not going to answer this phone and tell this guy to stay the hell away from my wife. So I click the button to accept the call.

"Hello, asshole," I say through my teeth.

There is a long pause on the other line. He's probably shocked Claudia didn't pick up and wondering if he should hang up. It doesn't matter. I'm going to find him either way.

"Who am I speaking to?" a voice says. It's a male voice,

deep and overly formal. It's not what I expected.

"I'm Claudia's husband," I say. "And you're busted. I want you to leave her alone from now on. You got me?"

Another long pause. "This is Robert Delaney?"

"Yeah. Who'd you think it was?"

A throat clears on the other line. "Mr. Delaney, this is Officer Higgins. We found this phone number on a burner phone in the pocket of your brother-in-law, Derek Alexander."

My world tilts sideways as my mouth drops open. "*What?*"

There is shuffling on the other line while I sit on the bed, gripping the phone so hard that it hurts my fingers. I've almost driven myself crazy by the time I hear another voice come on the line: "Mr. Delaney, this is Deputy Dwyer."

Scott Dwyer has been on the police force since I've lived here. As far as I know, he's a good man and a good cop. But none of that makes me feel any better.

"Deputy," I choke out. "What's going on?"

"Mr. Delaney, is this your phone?"

"No!" I burst out. "Christ, no. I found it."

"Found it where?"

The answer to this question is going to get Claudia in a world of trouble. But I can't lie. Even if I wanted to, I wouldn't.

"I found it in Claudia's dresser drawer."

There's another long silence on the other line. I can only imagine the conversation going on right now.

"Where are you, Mr. Delaney?" Dwyer finally says.

"I… I'm home."

"Is your wife there as well?"

"No…"

"Are you expecting her home soon?"

"I didn't even expect her not to be here." I let out a laugh that sounds strangled. "But yeah, I think she'll be home soon."

"Don't go anywhere, Mr. Delaney. I'm on my way."

———

My hair is still damp from the shower by the time Deputy Dwyer's police car pulls up in front of my house. Right after we hung up, I went down to the kitchen, poured myself a shot of scotch and downed it in one gulp. I should be sober for when I talk to the police, but the hell with it. I needed a drink.

It won't make me drunk. Just something to get my hands to stop shaking.

I'm already rising off the sofa when Dwyer makes it to the front door. I've got the door open half a second after he hits the doorbell. He's wearing his blue cop uniform, and I'm glad he doesn't try to shake my hand, because my palms are cold and damp.

"Hello, Mr. Delaney," he says. "Sorry to disturb you.

Can I come in?"

I wordlessly step aside to let him enter my home. Scott Dwyer is around thirty, with hair that looks reddish in the overhead lights of our living room. He looks like he might've had freckles when he was younger, but they've faded. Claudia once said in a disparaging kind of way that Quinn dated Scott Dwyer when they were in high school. She laughed when she talked about how Dwyer showed up at their door like a puppy dog, always searching for Quinn.

I wonder what Dwyer thinks happened to Derek Alexander. I wonder if he thinks Quinn killed him.

"Can I get you something to drink, Deputy?" I ask as I lead him to the sofa. I suddenly worry he can smell the scotch on my breath. "Water, I mean."

He shakes his head and settles down on the cushions of our worn blue sofa. "No, thanks."

I sit down on the loveseat across from him. Claudia is always saying we need new furniture. Every time she goes over to Quinn's house, she goes on a rant about how our stuff isn't as nice as theirs. But our stuff is fine. You don't have to own a ten thousand dollar leather sofa.

"So." I dig the phone out of my pocket and hold it out to him. "Here it is. If you want it."

Damn straight he wants it. He reaches for it, flips it open and stares at the screen. I sit there watching him as he scrolls through the text messages, the same way I did. I wait patiently, but I'm sitting on my hands. After a couple of minutes, he finally focuses his attention back on me. "Where did you find the phone?"

"I was putting away Claudia's laundry. I found it tucked between two shirts."

"So… it was hidden."

"Yeah." My jaw tightens. "You can see why."

"Yes," he says. "Did you suspect Claudia was having an affair at any point?"

"No. Never." Although now it makes me feel stupid to say it. I should have known. But how could I? I was too busy supporting my family. Digging rats out of pipes and all that crap.

"Were you and Claudia close with Derek and Quinn?"

"Claudia and Quinn were close." I cough into my hand. "Well, I thought they were."

"Do you think Claudia could have hurt Quinn?"

I frown. "Wait. Do you think Claudia might have been the one who stabbed Derek? And… done something to Quinn?"

Deputy Dwyer folds his arms across his chest. "We're just trying to explore every possibility."

"Oh," I breathe. "Yeah, okay. Makes sense."

"Do you think she might have, Mr. Delaney? Do you think she's capable of it?"

I reach out and touch the scar on my hairline. The one that required five stitches in the emergency room.

"Yes," I say. "She's capable of it."

CHAPTER 39

CLAUDIA

I had it all planned out perfectly yesterday.

I had a two o'clock massage client. And as soon as I finished with her, I was going to head over to Quinn's monstrosity of a house.

Except I wasn't going there to see my sister.

Yes, it's true. I've been sleeping with my sister's husband for the last six months. I should probably use the past tense, since Derek will not be sleeping with me anymore—never again—given that he's lying on a slab in the morgue. After she *murdered* him.

I can't even think about it. The sight of his dead body lying on the kitchen floor will be burned in my eyes forever.

That bitch.

Derek is superb in bed. Quinn never even mentioned that to me—she didn't even appreciate it. I started sleeping with him because… Well, long story short, I hate my sister.

Surprise, surprise.

I didn't always hate my sister. When our parents were alive and life was easy, we were close enough. But then they died—not just that, but they died on their way to *Quinn's* stupid play. And they left us with *nothing*.

I was at the end of my freshman year of college. I had plans. Of course I did. And none of those plans involved babysitting my sister for the next four years. I wanted to finish college and go on to law school. That was my dream since I was a kid. But after our parents died, Quinn had nobody. Our closest relative was a third cousin out in the Midwest. I figured she could go there and stay with her for a few years. Then our cousin called me and started making me feel guilty. She said she and her husband didn't have enough money and why couldn't I take care of her? *You are eighteen, after all. She's your own sister, for goodness sake.*

So I did it. I became Quinn's guardian. Naturally, I had to drop out of college. Get a minimum wage job and borrow money to keep from losing the house. All the while, Quinn went to high school, and then she went on to college. Meanwhile, I never found my way back to college. After four years out of the game, it felt like another world. So I got my degree in massage therapy instead. Married Rob.

It wasn't what I dreamed of. But it was good enough.

But then I saw Quinn living the good life. She finished college and got a good job at the bank. She met this obscenely gorgeous man, and he fell helplessly in love with her, because she's always been prettier than me. I used to be the *smart* one, but a fat lot of good it did me without an education to back it up.

Whenever I would see Quinn with Derek, I would think of the guy I got stuck with—the balding plumber—and feel a surge of jealousy. Why did her life have to work out so well and mine so badly?

Then she married Derek. They built this obscenely large house and spent a fortune furnishing the place. And all she did was complain about him. Because Derek was *mean* to her. Well guess what? Rob is mean to me too, and I don't get to live in a palace.

She just didn't get it. She didn't appreciate everything I gave up for her. She never even thanked me.

Last year, the roof of our house collapsed during a storm. Our attic filled with water, which then leaked down into our bedrooms. I remember standing outside the house with Quinn, showing her the damage.

"How awful!" she remarked.

"It's eating right through all the wood," I told her.

She frowned at me. "But you can fix it, right?"

"Yes, but it'll cost a bundle."

I stood there, waiting for her to offer to help. Derek

was rolling in money, and even Quinn earned four or five times as much as I did from my massage clients. "Well, at least you can fix it," she said.

That was it. No offer to help the sister that had sacrificed so much for her. And it wasn't the first time either. She always expected me to be there for her, but she was never there for me. When Rob got laid off a few years back, she took some trip off to Bermuda with her boyfriend. She never cared about me. It was always the Quinn Show.

Can you blame me for hating her? Wouldn't anyone?

You might wonder how I ended up sleeping with Derek. Like I said, Quinn is the pretty one. Why would Derek want to be with me when he already had the prettier, younger sister?

It happened when Quinn was away on a business trip. I had the key to her house, and she asked me to water her plants, because she knew Derek wouldn't do it. Of course, she could've hired somebody to water her goddamn plants instead of me making the trek all the way over and do it for her, but Quinn never thought about it like that. What better thing did I have to do than take care of her stupid overpriced plants?

While I was at her house, I helped myself to her wardrobe closet. Quinn had more clothes than she knew what to do with, and even though I was a couple sizes bigger, some of her stuff still fit me, like her jackets. And even if it didn't fit me, I might get a good price for it on eBay. She would never even know it was gone.

I was in the middle of trying on one of her Bottega Veneta jackets and admiring myself in the mirror, when I saw a reflection that made me nearly jump out of my skin. Derek was standing in the doorway, watching me.

"Oh, hi!" I quickly shrugged off the jacket and reached for a hanger. "I was just… you know…"

But there was no judgment on Derek's face. He smiled at me, and he looked so handsome at that moment, it made my knees weak. "It looks better on you."

I blushed like a teenager. I didn't think it was true, but his face looked sincere. "Thanks."

He came across the room, and my heart sped up. He reached out and straightened the collar of my shirt. His fingers lingered there, making a tingle go down my entire body. I held my breath, not sure what to make of this turn of events. Sometimes when I was visiting, Derek would flirt with me a bit or maybe wink suggestively. Truth be told, I had a crush on him. It was hard not to.

"You're a masseuse, right?" he said.

"Yes," I managed. Men rarely left me breathless, but there was something about Derek.

He rubbed at his shoulder. "You know, I have this terrible crick in my neck. I was wondering if you might take a look."

"I could do that." My body tingled at the thought of getting Derek on my massage table. "When do you have in mind?"

"How about right now?"

"I don't have my massage table."

His lips quirk up. "Couldn't we use the bed?"

I felt suddenly breathless, but I managed to nod. "Yes. We could."

I watched Derek strip down in front of me to his underwear. I've never seen my sister's husband naked before, and I have to say, he was spectacular. Like a sculpture. He lay down on the bed, face down. Waiting for me.

I rubbed my hands together to warm them. I didn't have any of my oils or lotions, so I ran my bare fingers along his broad shoulders. I started working the palms of my hands into his trapezius, kneading his taut muscles. He moaned at my touch.

"You're good at this," he commented.

"It's my special skill."

"Do you have any other special skills?"

Before I could answer, he rolled over. His eyes met mine, and my body melted. He sat up and pressed his lips against mine. I have never been kissed like that. Rob wasn't capable of it. Neither were any of the other men I had kissed in my life. Derek was different. I knew it right away.

That was the first time we ever had sex. In my sister's master bedroom, while she was away on a business trip.

At first, I was sleeping with Derek because I was wildly

attracted to him, and also to get back at my sister for all the sacrifices she never appreciated. But I got to really like him. After a session together, I didn't just throw my clothes back on and run out. We would lie together in bed, talking, for as long as we dared. He would run his fingers through my hair, staring into my eyes.

"I think I chose the wrong sister," he told me last week.

I whispered back, "It isn't too late, you know."

"If I left Quinn, would you leave Rob?"

I answered without hesitation: "I would."

I don't know if he meant it. I guess I'll never know. But at the time, I believed he did.

All afternoon yesterday, I was tingling with anticipation at the thought of seeing him, but then right after I sent my two o'clock packing, my boss came out and told me Heather had to go home sick. Any chance I could take Heather's three o'clock client?

As much as I wanted to see Derek, I couldn't say no. I needed the money too badly. It wasn't like my sister would lend me money if I needed it.

I sent Derek a regretful text message from the burner phone I bought so the two of us could communicate, letting him know I would be an hour late, maybe longer. Of course, if I came over there too late, I risked running into Quinn.

Although part of me wanted her to walk in on us. He told me he would leave her for me—well, that would force the issue. And I wanted to see the look on her face. She always thought she was better than me. How would she feel when she discovered that her wonderful, perfect husband preferred me to her?

When I finished up with Heather's client, I grabbed my burner phone. There were no messages from Derek, but I took no news as good news. Derek wasn't the kind of guy who felt the need to respond to every message. He wasn't needy.

But Quinn was an issue. I didn't want her walking in on us, considering it was getting late. So as I got into my car, I called her. The phone rang several times before she picked up.

"Hi, Claudia!" She sounded in a good mood. For a change. Quinn had been such a sad sack lately. I was so sick of hearing her complain incessantly about her perfect life.

"Quinn," I said, trying to sound casual. "Where are you? Are you free?"

"Not at the moment. I'm still at work."

A lie. She was not at work—I know that now. She was already on the run.

But I didn't know it back then, so I had to weasel her plans out of her. Find out how long Derek and I would have together. "What time do you get off? Do you want to grab dinner?"

"No, I… I have to work late tonight."

I tutted and made some comment about how hard they worked her, and of course, she agreed. Even though she had a totally cushy desk job. Try massaging somebody's muscles for six hours straight and see how you feel.

"Tell you what," I said. "How about if I come over tonight with a bottle of wine?"

"No!" She sounded freaked out about the idea of it, and now I was curious. At the time, I thought she and Derek must've had an argument. I was desperate for more details. "I mean… I've got a headache and I… it's not a good night. I don't feel like socializing."

I tried to get her to tell me, but she was resistant. "Fine," I said. "But you owe me dinner out. Tomorrow night, Rob and I are going out… how about Sunday?"

"How about Monday?"

"Deal. Let's meet at Donatello's at seven. Don't be late!"

Of course, she had no intention of meeting me on Monday. She expected to be long gone by then. She nixed the idea of doing Sunday because she didn't want me to walk in and discover her husband's body. She had no idea I was on my way to her house right then.

When I got to Quinn and Derek's house, my body was almost buzzing with anticipation the way it always was when I was about to see Derek. I had a key to the house, so I let myself in. Usually Derek met me at the door—I loved the sexy smile that would spread across his face when I walked in.

But this time, I didn't see him.

"Derek?" I called out. No answer.

I checked my phone, to make sure he hadn't texted me and told me not to come. But there was nothing.

"Derek?" I stepped into the living room, looking around. "Are you here?"

He didn't answer, so I went into the kitchen and…

I fell to my knees in front of his dead body. Yes, he was definitely dead. I didn't have any medical knowledge, but I could tell that much. He was lying in a pool of drying blood, his beautiful face chalky, his lips parted, his eyes cracked open. I thought of this man as being so full of life, and here he was, totally and utterly dead.

I picked up his hand, which already felt stiff. Vaguely, I knew that I shouldn't be touching things around what was clearly a crime scene. But I couldn't help myself. I loved this man.

And now he was dead. Just like my parents.

"Who did this to you?" I whispered.

Unsurprisingly, he did not answer.

I got to my feet. I scanned the first floor of the house. "Quinn!" I shrieked.

I went running from room to room, screaming Quinn's name. I wanted to smash everything in their beautiful house, but even through my haze of grief, I knew that would be stupid. Anyway, she was long gone by then.

I thought there was a tiny possibility that somebody had killed Derek and taken Quinn hostage. But I knew how

Quinn felt about him. I knew they fought constantly. Really, there was never any doubt in my mind that she was the one who stabbed him to death.

I also knew she would get away with it. Okay, she was stupid to run—that would hurt her case. But she would use some sort of defense about how he abused her, and she'd get off scot free. He *wasn't* abusive to her. I know how Quinn can be. Sometimes I wanted to smack her upside the head myself.

I had to find Quinn. And then I promised myself I would make her pay for what she had done to the man I loved.

I triple dipper promised with a cherry on top.

It was lucky I found her phone before the police did. It helped that Deputy Scotty Dwyer was such an idiot. I attempted to throw them off her trail, but it didn't work. Quinn was too careless and managed to get herself pulled over. She couldn't even do that part right. Even our hopelessly incompetent police force would find her at this rate.

So I went after her. To the Baxter Motel.

When I parked in the lot, the motel looked almost deserted. The lights were off in all the rooms. It looked like nobody had stayed there in years. For a moment, I thought I had made a mistake. Maybe Quinn hadn't come here after all.

But then I saw her bursting from the front door. She

was dragging her luggage behind her, and there were tears in her eyes. She was making a quick getaway, that's for sure. If I had shown up one minute later, I would have missed her entirely. The timing could not have been better.

I dug around in my purse until I found Rob's pocket knife. I left my purse behind and got out of the car, gripping the knife in my right hand.

"Hi, Quinn!" I called out.

She looked up at me in surprise. She never expected to see me again. But she didn't look upset. Of course not. I'm her big sister. The one who always bails her out of trouble. She probably thought I was here to help.

Ha.

"Thank God, Claudia!" she sobbed.

She started towards me and tried to embrace me, but I took a step back. She blinked, surprised by my rebuff.

"Claudia?" she said.

"How could you?" I choked out. "How could you do that?"

"He…" Her hands flew to her neck. "He was trying to choke me. I… I had to…"

"Liar!" I hissed at her. "You couldn't stand it that he liked me better."

"Claudia, what are you talking about?"

"You know exactly what I'm talking about."

And then her eyes widened as she saw the knife in my right hand. She finally got it. She knew Derek was fooling around on her, but she never knew it was with me. But now, moments before her death, she knew. I wanted her to know.

And then I plunged the knife into her abdomen and dug it in, the same way she did to him. Poetic justice.

Quinn's body crumbled to the ground. My sister had always been petite, and in recent years she's become downright skeletal—whereas my arms are taut and muscular from my work as a masseuse—so I easily heaved her limp body into my arms and lowered it into the open trunk of my car.

It was only after slamming the trunk closed that I saw the light go on in the second floor of the motel.

A witness.

My stomach clenched at the idea that someone might have seen what I had just done. I shouldn't have been so careless. I should have invited her into my car, taken her somewhere else, and done it there.

That was always my problem. I acted without thinking.

So I went into the motel to get a room. There was no way there were more than one or two people staying there. I had to tie up the loose ends. And I needed to kill a little time anyway, since the police were still circling the area. I would take care of what I needed to take care of here, then by the time I left with Quinn's body in the trunk, the police would have moved on.

Except then Greta made me aware of one other witness I hadn't thought about. The woman on the second floor of that broken down old house. *Rosalie*.

She's the last loose end.

As soon as I take care of her, I can go.

———

I don't know if Rosalie called the police already. Maybe she did and it's too late. But based on the fact that Rob couldn't hear a word I was saying when he called me, I'm betting she wasn't able to call anyone. Maybe she's waiting for the cell reception to return. It will be too late for her by then.

I read about her in one of the articles. Rosalie Baxter. According to the article, she is "confined to a wheelchair." Much like Greta, she'll go down easy.

Nick Baxter—he won't go down as easy. But he's busy in Room 201, repairing that leak. He won't see a thing. Best of all, after that mess two years ago, if another person is murdered under his watch, he'll definitely get nailed for it. Everyone already thinks he's a killer. It won't be much of a stretch. Nick Baxter will take the fall for everything I've done.

It's all too perfect.

As I walk up the steps to the bedroom overlooking the hotel, the knife feels heavy in my hand. I never would have thought I could do something like this, but somehow it gets easier each time. I wonder if it was easy for Quinn too. When she put that knife in Derek's belly.

My heart aches when I think about it. I can't believe

he's dead. I can't believe he'll never hold me again.

And then I'm there—in the master bedroom. I put my hand on the doorknob. I thought I might be shaky, but I'm not. I don't know what Rosalie Baxter has in store for me behind the door. Yes, she might be in a wheelchair, but that doesn't mean she doesn't have a gun. I could open the door and she could shoot me right in the face.

Somehow, I don't think she will. And strangely enough, I'm not scared.

I throw open the door, and there she is, sitting in her wheelchair. I was right to have not been scared. As ominous as she looked when she was a shadow in the window, Rosalie Baxter is absolutely non-threatening up close. She's tiny—not much taller than five feet if she could stand, and bone thin, almost like a corpse. Her brown eyes are enormous on her skinny face as she stares up at me.

I hardly even need a knife. I could snap her in half with my bare hands. Hell, it looks like a strong breeze might do her in.

I'll be doing her a favor. This woman must have a miserable life. Stuck up here all alone all day, unable to move. Having to live with that crabby husband of hers, who's probably been sleeping with every pretty girl who walks through the door. I'll end it quick for her.

But she looks terrified. She holds up her hands, which are shaking. "I'm sorry," she gasps. "Whatever you think I did, I'm sorry."

Her eyes dart to the side, and I realize what's on the bed. It's a pair of binoculars. She's been watching me through binoculars. How pathetic. And sneaky. All my sympathy for this wretched creature has vanished—maybe I won't make it quick.

Good thing I came here.

"You know what happened to my sister," I snap at her.

She blinks her giant brown eyes. "Your... sister?"

I take a step towards her and she flinches. "Don't play dumb."

"I... I don't know what you're talking about..."

"Liar..."

"Please..." Now she's sobbing. "I didn't do anything to your sister. I *swear*."

"I never said you did." My shoulders tense with aggravation. Why is she pretending? Does she think I'm that stupid? "But I know what you saw."

Her delicate jaw trembles. "Saw?"

"You and your binoculars..." I sneer at her. "You're pathetic."

She flinches, her face turning pink. "I'm so sorry. I shouldn't have... I'm so *sorry*..."

"It's too late."

"No. *No*. Please.... You can't..." She looks down at her phone, a pathetically hopeful expression on her face. "Nick will come. You won't get away with it..."

"No," I say, "he won't come." Then I drop the

bombshell on her. I reach into my purse with my free hand and pull out the phone I swiped from the front desk. "Because I have his phone."

What little color she still had in her face drains away. She knows she's screwed. I've got the knife and her husband's phone and she's got nothing. Nobody is coming for her.

It's all over for Rosalie Baxter.

CHAPTER 40

ROSALIE

I still had that one last hope. The hope that Nick would get my text and come running. He would be there for me like he always has been.

But when that horrible woman shows me my husband's cell phone, that hope vanishes. And more than anything, I'm terrified to know how she got that phone. What did she do to Nick to get it?

"Oh, don't worry," she laughs. "Nick is fine. He left it on the front desk and I took it with me." She cocks her head to the side. "Well, he's fine for now. But he's definitely going to jail for killing you. I'll be long gone by then."

As she closes in on me, I feel like I'm choking. She can't

get away with this, can she?

But maybe she can. After all, Nick only just escaped being charged with Christina Marsh's murder two years ago. If I'm found murdered, there's no way they won't charge him. He'll go to jail for this. Maybe forever.

I can't die this way. I can't. Nick and I are supposed to have a happy ending. Greta said so! I'm sick of feeling sorry for myself. If I live through this, I'm going to appreciate every moment I've got left.

That choking feeling intensifies, and I cough. As the sound leaves my mouth, the woman flinches. She looks concerned. It occurs to me she doesn't know what's wrong with me. She has no idea why I'm sick. For all she knows, I'm highly contagious.

So I start coughing more.

She freezes. I should probably be dead by now, but she's not sure what to do. My coughing has thrown her for a loop. If I'm going to do anything, now is the time. Because it's clear Nick isn't coming.

So I gather every ounce of my strength. And I lunge at her.

For a moment, the world is a dizzying roller coaster. I wasn't sure if I would have the bulk to do it, but somehow, I managed to topple her over, and then the two of us fall to the ground. There's a loud cracking sound as her skull hits the floor. I don't know if she's still got the knife or not, but I'm not going to check. I reach out and run my fingernails down the side of her face.

She screams. It's been a while since I've cut them, I guess.

She's got to have the upper hand on me, because I've been rotting away in this room for the last several years so I'm weak as a kitten. But the adrenaline rush of almost being stabbed to death has given me back some strength. I don't even think about it. I'm scratching and clawing at her with every fiber of my being. If she wants to kill me, I won't make it easy for her. And I'm going to get plenty of her DNA under my fingernails so they'll know it wasn't Nick who did this to me.

"Whoa! Jesus Christ, Rosie!"

I pause for a breath and look up. Nick is standing over us, gawking at me. I look down at the mystery woman under me, and there's blood all over her face. I think she might be unconscious. I roll off her, gasping for air.

"Nick," I manage. "She… she was…"

"I know." His face is grim. "I saw her through the window in room 201. I saw the knife. I ran over here as fast as I could, but I thought I might be too late…" He looks down at the woman, out cold on the floor. "Little did I know, my wife is a ninja."

I start to laugh, but instead I burst into tears.

CHAPTER 41

CLAUDIA

When I come to, I'm lying on the floor.

For a moment, I'm too disoriented to know what happened. All I remember is that sick woman coughing all over me, like she was about to die. And then a second later, she was knocking me to the ground. I couldn't believe the force in that little body. She was clawing at my face, and then everything went black.

I blink my eyes, and a sharp jab of pain stabs me in the back of the head. I can't believe she knocked me down like that.

The room gradually comes into focus, and I realize I'm not alone. That guy Nick is sitting on the bed, my knife in his hand. His lips are set in a straight line.

"Don't move," he says. "The police are on their way."

I look at his eyes, which are like ice. He means what he says. After all, he's already killed somebody. His mistress.

"Look." I struggle to sit up. "You don't have to turn me over to the police. Nobody got hurt."

His eyes flash. "I told you not to move."

I take a deep breath. I've got nothing to lose. He doesn't know this, but if he doesn't let me out of this room in the next minute, I'm finished. "I can give you money. Whatever you want."

He just snorts.

Fine. "You know," I say, "really, it's your word against mine. I gingerly touch my face, covered in his wife's scratch marks. My hand comes away wet with my blood. "I'm the one who's hurt here. I'll tell the police you attacked me. You and your nut job wife. Both of you will go to jail."

Nick doesn't react to that.

"Just let me go." I shift on the floor, ready to scramble to my feet if he lets me. "Let me leave now and I won't tell anyone. I swear."

"If you move again," he says calmly, "I will put this knife through your eye. Got it, lady?"

"I'll tell them you threatened me," I say in a small voice. "You're doing it right now. You're threatening me. Who do you think they'll believe?"

Nick stares at me for a moment, his shoulders rising

and falling with each breath. "I saw what you did to Greta," he hisses at me. "And you tried to kill my wife. If you think I'm *ever* letting you leave this room except in handcuffs, you're out of your mind."

Oh. He knows about the old lady. Damn.

And now I hear the sirens, growing louder by the second. Nick is gripping the knife so hard, his knuckles are white. Just a short time ago, I was the one with a knife, and Rosalie was cowering in front of me. She lunged at me and took me down. But I can take one look at Nick and know that I won't be able to do the same to him. He will absolutely kill me if I try to get up off the floor.

A few minutes later, the police descend on us. Someone must've told them the entire story on the phone, because it seems like they know everything. They handcuff me and read me my rights, even though my face is bleeding and my head is throbbing.

They lead me down the stairs, and outside into the cold. I took my jacket off when I came into the house, but they don't give me a chance to retrieve it. I suppose I've lost the right to a jacket.

As I come out of the house, I see they have jimmied open the trunk of my car. Deputy Scott Dwyer is standing there, right next to the trunk, and when it pops open, his face turns green.

"Oh, Christ," Scott says. "Where the hell is that ambulance?"

I know what they have discovered in my trunk. I stop walking abruptly, surprising the officer whose hand is on my elbow, leading me to the police car. He stumbles and releases my arm. I sprint in the direction of my car.

No, I won't be able to get away. But I want to see.

It's Scott who jumps in front of me, just as another officer grabs me roughly by the arm. I always thought Scott was far too nice to be a cop, but at this moment, his eyes are like ice. He looks like he could strangle me with his bare hands.

"How could you?" he chokes out. "How could you do that to her? You…"

I stare back at him. "Sorry, Scotty. You missed your chance with her."

His right hand balls into a fist. He wants to hit me. It says a lot about him that he doesn't do it, even though I'm an easy target with my hands cuffed behind my back. He's still a wuss. He won't even do anything when he sees the girl he's had a crush on for ten years bleeding to death in the trunk of a car.

"Is she breathing?" I ask.

Scott just sneers at me. He nods his head at the officer holding my arm. "Take her away."

I start to ask again, but I feel my arm being jerked hard enough that my wrist feels like it might snap in two. I know the answer though. Quinn will survive. She's the lucky one, after all.

CHAPTER 42

ROSALIE

It feels like the police are with us forever.

Nick carried me downstairs, so I wouldn't have to deal with being near that woman. Her name, apparently, is Claudia Delaney. She's the sister of the other woman who was staying here—the one who kissed Nick. I still don't entirely understand why Claudia Delaney stabbed her sister, but apparently, they found her unconscious and bleeding profusely in the trunk of Claudia's car. They rushed her to the hospital, but they're not sure if she'll survive. I can't even imagine.

The police spend forever talking to Nick. I can tell he's trying hard to keep his cool, going over the same story again and again. And he's really upset about Greta. He went into her room to tell her to call the police, and he found her lying on the ground, a stab wound in her chest. We had both grown very fond of her. Amazingly, she was still breathing when the paramedics arrived. But she was quite old—her chances aren't great.

Finally the police leave, and thank God, they haven't hauled my husband away in handcuffs. He sinks into one of the chairs at our dining room table, his face pale. I wheel over to him, afraid to ask him what he's thinking. After all, we broke up. A few hours ago, we decided our marriage was done. As far as I know, he's already checked out.

"Nick," I say.

He lifts his eyes, which are red-rimmed. "Hey."

"Are you… okay?"

"Yeah, I…" He heaves a sigh. "She almost killed you. I can't believe it."

I try to smile. "Nah. I was fine. I took her down, no problem."

"You did, didn't you?" He tries to return the smile. "Listen, Rosie…"

I brace myself. I don't want to hear this. I don't want him to tell me he's leaving me tonight. I don't think I could bear it after the night I've had.

No, he might not leave tonight. But he's going to want to make plans for separating. I don't know if I can talk him out of it anymore. This decision has been a long time coming.

But I'll try.

"I want to stay together," he blurts out.

I stare at him. "You do?"

"Yeah." He rubs his eyes with the balls of his hands, then looks back up at me. "I was miserable after our conversation earlier. I don't want to live without you. *Ever.* I'm sad about… the way things are. With us. But I'm not giving up. I love you too much."

"Oh," I say.

"And," he adds, "I think you still love me too."

My cheeks grow warm. "You're right. I do. I really, really do."

He reaches out and takes my hand in his. "I knew it."

"Also," I say, "I think this dining room would make a really great bedroom."

For the first time, maybe in years, I see his eyes light up. "I think so too."

And so we sit there for the next hour, holding hands, and making plans for the future.

EPILOGUE

QUINN

Two and a Half Years Later

It's a hot lazy Sunday afternoon.

Temperatures are up in the nineties today. Rightfully, I should be inside my house, with the air conditioner cranked up. But ever since my short stint in prison, I hate to be indoors for very long. So this morning, when it was cooler, I did some gardening. I sold our ostentatious house last year, and I purchased something much smaller with a beautiful garden in the back. I get so much joy out of working on it.

And now I'm celebrating my morning of labor by

sitting on my front porch, in a rocking chair, having a delicious glass of lemonade with lots of ice in it. It's the late afternoon and the temperatures will drop soon. A slight breeze lifts a few stray strands of hair off the back of my neck.

Some days, it's just nice to be alive.

I almost wasn't. I shift in the rocking chair, aware of that tight feeling in my abdomen that I get when I'm in certain positions. I will always have a scar there to remind me of how I almost lost my life. How I was in critical condition in the hospital, a tube down my throat.

All because of Claudia. My sister.

I felt so stupid when I found out. I had no idea how much she had grown to resent me over the years. I certainly never suspected she was the one sleeping with my husband. Or that she was *in love* with him.

I still wouldn't believe it if she hadn't said it to my face. When I tried to offer her money for her legal defense, she turned it down. *Don't do me any favors. You never have.*

I wish she had taken the money. Her lawyer tried to use an insanity defense, citing Claudia's uncontrolled bipolar disorder. I knew about the diagnosis, but I thought her illness was controlled with medication—apparently, she had stopped taking it, and poor Rob had no idea. Anyway, the defense didn't work. The jury convicted her of three charges of attempted murder. She's going to be in jail for a very long time.

I've tried to visit her, but she refuses to see me.

Fortunately, I hired a talented lawyer for my own defense. It was somebody Scott Dwyer recommended to me. And that man from the motel, Nick Baxter, testified on my behalf about the bruises on my neck. He ended up being a really good guy in the end. I was acquitted of all charges when the jury ruled I had acted in self-defense.

I take a gulp of lemonade just as the police car pulls up in front of my house. It took a while before the sight of a police car stopped making me feel sick. It's a side effect of having been on trial for murder. But now that I'm dating a police officer, I've learned to get over it.

Scott Dwyer emerges from the car, a big grin on his face. His face always lights up at the sight of me. And he's changed out of his police uniform into a nice white dress shirt and pants. He looks achingly handsome.

For a long time, I couldn't even contemplate being in a relationship with another man. After the trial was over, I swore off men for good. But Scott stayed by my side during the entire trial and in the aftermath, giving me advice whenever he could. Nothing ever happened between us, but he was the first friend I'd had in a long time. Derek would never have let me be friends with a man, but now I was free to do what I wanted.

Then about three months ago, on a hot day like this one, Scott suggested we go get some ice cream.

And now we are a couple.

"You ready to go?" Scott asks me.

I rise from the rocking chair and brush out a few wrinkles in my blue sundress. I tuck a stray strand of my dark hair behind my ears. I haven't dyed my hair in two and a half years, and it has finally grown in its natural color. I missed it.

"Ready," I say.

He glances at his watch. "It should take about an hour to get there. Not much traffic."

I smile at him. "I'm not in a rush."

I step down the walkway to his car. He dashes around the side of the vehicle so he can open the door for me. I always tell him he doesn't have to do it, but he wants to. It's sweet.

"The reviews for the restaurant are phenomenal," Scott remarks as he slides into the driver seat. "I can't wait. You're sure we're going to get a table?"

"I'm sure," I say. "I called ahead."

Scott reaches out to give my hand a squeeze. Then he starts the engine and we're on our way. I don't know if he is going to be the man I end up with, but I'm happy with him now. He treats me right, and I like him a lot. And that's what's important to me right now.

And in one hour, we're going to have a lovely dinner at Rosalie's. Nick promised he'd save a table for us.

ROSALIE

Rosalie's is busy tonight.

Of course, it's busy every night these days. The restaurant went from being boarded up to eventually getting a steady stream of business, and last month, Nick got us a write up in a popular food blog, and now it's gotten *crazy* busy. It can be a little stressful, but I love it.

A new waitress, Vanessa, comes to the pass with two new tables full of order tickets. Vanessa just started last month, but she's been doing a good job. I reach for the tickets from the counter, which we had lowered to accommodate a person who can't stand. The entire kitchen has been modified for me, although we left a lot of it the same because I'm running the kitchen and not doing the cooking anymore. I make sure every plate that leaves the kitchen is up to my standards. This isn't just a side of the road diner. This is something better—something special. Or at least, I like to think it is.

"Everyone is enjoying their food?" I ask Vanessa.

She nods eagerly. "The tips are amazing tonight."

I laugh. "Glad to hear it."

After I call out the new tickets for my little brigade of cooks, I look up and see Nick standing at the entrance to the kitchen. He grins at me and gives me a little wave. "Is this a bad time?"

I let out an exaggerated sigh. "It's always a bad time. Why do you have to be so good at publicizing this place?"

"I don't know. Why do you have to be so good a chef?"

I fold my arms across my chest, resting on my belly. "You're the one at fault. I'm pretty sure."

"Yeah, yeah." He cocks his head to the side. "How are you feeling?"

"I'm fine."

"Are you sure because—"

"I'm *fine*, Nick." I give him a look. "Stop worrying."

"Sorry," he says sheepishly. "But... I just can't wait, you know?"

Nick doesn't usually fret about me this way. Ever since that night I almost died, he's pushed me like crazy. More than I wanted to be pushed some days. We went back to Dr. Heller and got me on some medications that helped a lot with my fatigue. And one that helped a lot with my depression as well. I should have taken the anti-depressants to begin with—I had no clue how dark my life had become until the fog lifted. And I got a power wheelchair to use outside of the house, so I didn't have to use all my energy pushing myself around when fatigue was already an issue.

Once the depression was gone, I felt like myself again. And I couldn't believe I had almost let my dreams slip away from me.

So the two of us set about getting it back. It was slow going the first year, but like last time, it eventually took off.

This is the busiest Rosalie's has ever been. We have people waiting for tables most nights.

So the timing couldn't be worse. But is the timing ever perfect to have a baby? It doesn't matter. Because like it or not, in one short month, Nick and I are going to be parents.

After what happened last time, I can't entirely blame him for worrying. And this is a terrible time for me to be taking a maternity leave. One of my cooks is going to step up to help with expediting, but because funds are still tight, Nick is going to do it on the typically slower nights. I've been training him, and he's actually not too bad at it. He might not be able to cook, but he knows good food. And he's very organized and forceful when he needs to be.

"I can't wait either." I rest a hand on my baby bulge, which has gotten more and more unwieldy in the last couple of months. "But don't worry. I'm okay. I promise."

He crouches down next to me. He rests one of his hands on top of mine on my belly, then leans in and kisses me. I should be pushing out orders now, but it's hard to resist my husband. After five years of essentially living like strangers, it's like we're on a new honeymoon.

It just took almost dying.

In the weeks after the incident, we finally got all the details, although it was mostly from reading them in the paper. The woman who showed up earlier in the night, Quinn Alexander, had just murdered her husband. She stabbed him in the belly, although there was significant evidence that she did it in self-defense. Nick told the police he saw bruises on her neck, and he assumed somebody had attacked her. Nick later ended up testifying in Quinn's trial.

But it turned out that the husband was sleeping with Quinn's sister, Claudia Delaney. And when the sister—apparently already a bit mentally unstable—discovered the dead body, she had a complete breakdown. Claudia set about finding Quinn, then exacting revenge on her. She stabbed Quinn, then put her in the trunk of her car, intending to get rid of the dead body.

And she went after me because she thought I saw her stabbing her sister. She was getting rid of the witnesses.

She did the same to Greta. After the old woman told her what she wanted to know, Claudia took care of her—stabbed her in the abdomen just like Quinn. But amazingly, the knife missed any major organs and Greta survived—she was home from the hospital within a week. She must have nine lives.

"Hey," Nick says to me now. "I know you're busy, but do you want to let me take over for half an hour so you can say goodbye to Greta?"

"Now?"

He shrugs. "She's leaving in the morning. She's got an early flight, so if you don't see her now, you might miss her."

After she recovered from her nearly fatal injuries, Greta got this idea in her head that she wanted to travel the world. *I don't have much time left. I want to see everything.* At first I thought she had forgotten about the whole thing, but then a few months ago, she told us she had booked plane tickets. Her flight is at seven in the morning tomorrow.

I look doubtfully at the tickets in the window. "Are you sure you can handle it??"

"Go! I promise, I'll be fine."

To prove his point, Nick strides over to the pass and starts expertly studying the tickets and making sure that all the plates are up to standard. He winks at me, and I smile back. I suppose it won't hurt to be gone for half an hour.

As I pass through the restaurant, I see Quinn Alexander sitting at one of the tables with her boyfriend—one of the police officers who had been involved in the case. Nick told me she had asked him to set aside a table for tonight. The two of them are holding hands across the table, and he's looking into her eyes. They look really happy. Good for them. After what she's been through, she deserves a happy ending.

The latest bit of construction Nick did was making sure the path from the restaurant back to the motel was paved, so it would be easy for my power wheelchair to glide across. I can't lie—doing everything I used to do before has been a challenge, but Nick has done everything he can to make sure the transition has been as smooth as possible. I'm lucky to have him. Although he claims he's lucky to have me. Maybe we're both lucky.

One thing we can't do is make the second floor of the motel accessible to me. The cost of putting in an elevator would be prohibitive, and it's not like I need to go up there anyway. And the lobby is beautiful now. Nick put in new carpeting last year that's a striking royal blue. He also patched up the ceiling after we fixed the leak in room 201. It's an interesting story—the husband of that woman, Claudia, came by to talk to us soon after her arrest, to offer an apology and explanation for what his wife had done. But when he noticed the leak, he offered to go up and fix it free of charge. Apparently, he's a plumber. That pipe had been leaking on and off for years, and the rust from the pipes turned the water brown—almost red—staining the ceiling. Fortunately, it hasn't leaked again since he fixed it, and we got the stain on the ceiling repainted. Robert Delaney knows what he's doing.

That said, we still haven't had any guests in Room 201. Nick still keeps the room closed all the time with the "DO NOT DISTURB" sign on the door. Eventually, he'll have to open it up, but he's not ready yet.

When I wheel into the lobby, Greta is already waiting for me. She is sitting in a wooden chair, wearing a dress rather than one of her many nightgowns with a long black coat over it. I almost don't recognize her in normal clothing.

"Let me guess," I say. "Your psychic premonition told

you I was coming."

She laughs. "No. Nick said you were going to stop by."

"Ah."

She tilts her head. "You look beautiful tonight, Rosalie. You're glowing."

I roll my eyes. "My pregnancy glow?"

"Pregnancy… love…" She reaches for my hand, and I let her take it. Her fingers are so frail and spidery. I can't believe she survived being stabbed in her belly—Nick and I thought for sure she was a goner. But she told me she had survived much worse. "You and Nick are going to live happily ever after. I told you. I told you there was happiness in your future."

I remember when she said that to me. I let her tell my fortune, and she told me those exact words. And I laughed at the time, because I couldn't imagine a happy future for myself. Yet here I am.

"I guess you really have a gift," I say.

"I will tell you a secret, Rosalie." Her fingers linger on mine. "I cannot really read the future. Or the past. I am just an ordinary woman."

"*Really.*" There's a note of sarcasm in my voice, but I'm a little surprised by her admission. Not that I ever believed in that stuff, but sometimes Greta did seem truly clairvoyant. After all, she predicted a happy ending for me and Nick when it seemed impossible.

"Yes. It is true."

"Well." I shrug. "It looks like your prediction about me and Nick came true after all."

"Yes. It did. Of course, I had to help it along."

"Help it along?"

She hesitates as her watery blue eyes stare into mine. "Rosalie, I want you to know that I never had children. And I always thought of you like a daughter. I wanted you to be happy."

"Yes…"

"Nick would have left you," she says. "That girl, Christina… she was a vixen. She set her sights on him—she *wanted* him. And no offense, my dear, but you were not doing much to hold on to him. You were delivering him to her on a silver platter! She told me how she thought Nick would be better off without you."

My mouth falls open. I didn't know about any of this. I had always assumed it was a fling—not that I asked for many details.

"So you see," she says, "I had to do what I did."

I pull my hand away from hers. "What did you do?"

"I saved your marriage!"

"Greta…" I feel a cramping sensation in my lower abdomen. "*What did you do?*"

Greta's blue eyes are wide. "She deserved it. Look at what she did. Fooling around with a married man. I'm disappointed in Nick too, but I understand what he was going through. She had no excuse. Terrible person."

My stomach turns. "Greta, you didn't…"

"She barely felt a thing." Greta strokes her long white hair. "I got the key from where Nick keeps them downstairs, and I let myself into her room during the night. I did it while she was sleeping. She only woke up for a minute, and it was too late by then. Nothing anyone could do."

All these years, I had been scared Nick was the one who killed Christina Marsh. I should have known he would never do something like that.

But I never dreamed Greta could have done it either.

"I've done it before." She says it casually, like she's talking about going roller skating instead of committing a murder. "There was a woman at the carnival who wanted my Bernie. And then she just… disappeared. That's what the police decided anyway."

I clasp a hand over my mouth. "Oh God…"

"I was trying to get rid of the other one for you too," she says. "Quinn. When she was downstairs, I looked through her bag, found out her real name. Then I said all the scary stuff about how she was in horrible danger. Left a few threatening messages for her in the Bible in the drawer. Got her on the run. Of course, it turned out she *was* in horrible danger."

"Greta…"

"Rosalie." She reaches for my hand again, but I yank it away. "Are you feeling poorly? You look so pale. It's not the baby, is it?"

"No, I…" But that cramp hits me again. Still, I've got an entire month to go. I'm not in labor. I'm just having a panic attack that a woman is dead because of me. "Greta, how could you do something like that?"

She blinks at me. "I did it for you, Rosalie." Her eyes darken. "If I hadn't, you would have none of this! He would have left you. No restaurant, no baby. Christina wanted him. You did not meet that woman. She thought I was on her side so she confided in me."

"She… did?"

"You do not know how she spoke about you. Nick's invalid wife. Frigid—won't even touch him. He deserves better. That's what she used to say."

Those Tarot cards were right all those years ago about my future. *Death.* Because Nick and I got married, a woman is dead. But he wasn't the one who killed her. It was *Greta.*

Greta reaches deep into the pocket of her long black wool coat. She pulls out a rectangular sign with the familiar words "DO NOT DISTURB" stenciled on it. She holds it out to me.

"I took this off the door of Room 201," she says. "It's time to open the room up again to guests. Let the past be the past."

I take the sign from her, but it drops from my fingers and flutters to the ground, the letters of "DO NOT DISTURB" staring up at me, looming before my eyes. I lean forward as my head spins. I get that cramping sensation one more time. I can't believe what I'm hearing. Greta killed a woman. I can't just pretend I didn't hear this. I have to call the police. I have to tell them what I know.

"You do not look well, Rosalie." She purses her lips. "Are you sure it's not the baby? Should I fetch Nick?"

"No, I…" But before I can protest, I feel this strange popping sensation inside me. I look down at the growing stain on my skirt. "Greta…"

"Your water broke!" She claps her hands together. "How exciting! I'll go get Nick."

I watch her run off to the restaurant to get my husband. My head is spinning. I'm about to have a baby. I'm in labor.

But I've got to call the police. I've got to tell them that Greta killed Christina Marsh. I can't let her get away with murder, even if she did it for me.

Where is my phone? Where did I put it?

It seems like less than a minute later, Nick is dashing into the motel. His face is pale, but he's grinning. "Greta said you're in labor. She said your water broke. Are you okay?"

"I'm okay, but…" I take a breath. "Nick, my phone…"

"Don't worry about your phone. I've got mine. Come on, the hospital bag is in my trunk."

"But I need to—"

"Rosie, we have to go!" His eyes are shining. "Come on—let's get you to the hospital and have this baby!" He reaches over and wraps his arms around me. "I can't wait. I love you so much, Rosie."

"Where's Greta?" I say.

"She said she had to go. She ended up getting a flight late tonight and had to run, but she said to tell you that you're going to be a wonderful mother."

I'll look up at him, my head throbbing. Another cramp seizes my lower abdomen. I've got to get to the hospital—he's right. There's no time to call the police now. And by the time I do, Greta will be out of the country.

She planned it this way. She knew that if she told me, I would feel compelled to report her. She didn't tell me until the last second for that reason. But she wanted me to know. She wanted me to know that everything I have is because of her. She's right—Nick very well might have left me for Christina. If she hadn't done what she did, I wouldn't have him anymore. I wouldn't be on my way to the hospital, about to have my first child. I might not even be alive.

It was wrong that she murdered that woman. She should never have done it. But I can't say I'm sorry. And at that moment, I decide.

If we have a girl, we will name her Greta.

THE END

ACKNOWLEDGMENTS

I have to be honest—I often don't read the acknowledgments in books. Since I started writing, I have learned that I'm in the minority on this. A lot of people read the acknowledgments. In fact, I can think of at least three people who will buy a copy of this book, and go straight to the acknowledgments without reading even one other word first. (Hi, Dad!)

So it's a lot of pressure to make this entertaining in some way. Especially since I'm kind of just thanking the same people each time. Harper Lee only had to write like one acknowledgment every 60 years or so. I'm jealous of Harper Lee.

First, thank you to my mother and her amazing tendency toward hyperbole. ("This is the greatest book I've ever read! I can't stop crying!") Thank you to Kate, for the positive supportive feedback. Thanks to Rebecca, for your great advice (and good luck!). Thanks to Nelle, for your thorough and thoughtful advice (and also, did you know you have the same first name as Harper Lee?). Thanks to Rhona, for always being ready to look at another cover. Thanks to Mel, for not wanting to look at another cover but doing it anyway. Thanks to my amazing writing group.

And thank you to my husband. You may not read my books, but I'm glad you know the proper perspective for the words "Do Not Disturb" on a slightly oblique doorknob.

CRUCIAL PROBLEMS
IN CHRISTIAN PERSPECTIVE

BOOKS BY HENLEE H. BARNETTE
PUBLISHED BY THE WESTMINSTER PRESS

Crucial Problems in Christian Perspective
The New Theology and Morality